Walk, Trot, Die

Susan Kiernan-Lewis

Published by San Marco Press

Other books by Susan Kiernan-Lewis:
Fear of Falling
Murder on the Côte d'Azure
Murder à la Carte
Murder in Provence
The French Women's Diet
Horse Crazy after Forty
Air Force Brat
Grave Mistake
Life After Paris

Chapter One

1

La Bon Chance Farms was the oldest horse farm still operating in North Georgia.

Tucked away in a private pocket of countryside forty miles north of downtown Atlanta, the riding stable was an oasis of winding trails, peekaboo ponds and rolling pastures along the banks of the Chattahoochee.

Until two years ago, the farm had been the headquarters of the regional fox-hunting brigade, but the encroaching tract-house developments and strip malls had prompted the pony clubs and hunt clubs to relocate fifty miles away, outside of Athens. Bon Chance stood alone now, a relic of the times when Atlanta was known more for its Southern charm than its episodes of road-rage and killer crime rate.

White-slat fences crisscrossed the farm's five hundred acres of pastures, woods and river front, separating mares from geldings, polo fields from hacking trails, pasture from woods. A thin electrified wire threaded the top of the fences to discourage cribbing from some of the more bored inmates.

Barb-wire fencing, normally never used around horses, was used at Bon Chance on certain spots along the Chattahoochee River where the riding trails wandered too close to the water's edge. The banks were steep and pitched. A horse or two had fallen over.

"Jilly! Is this yours? I found it in the manure pile in the east pasture."

A tall woman, blonde and tan, strode up to the tie-up pole under a cluster of birch trees, waving a tattered riding crop. The woman, large-bottomed, with a cheerful face, wore expensive, if dirty, cotton riding breeches and a silk blouse open at the throat. She marched in dusty black riding boots to where a small, petite woman with dark hair stood next to a saddled mixed-breed Clydesdale.

"You're kidding," the smaller woman said, slapping a long-nailed hand to her hip and giving the Clydesdale's bridle a snappish tug. "Someone threw my crop in the shit-hole?"

Margo Sherman, barn manager at Bon Chance Farm, held out the crop to Jilly.

"Well, I don't know if anyone *threw*--"

"Don't be stupid, Margo! How do you *think* the damn thing got there?" Jilly Travers did not reach for the proffered crop. "Someone threw it there."

"Well, look, do you want it or not?"

Behind them, a pair of riders emerged from the main barn leading their mounts. The two approaching women were dressed in boots and breeches with their black velvet riding caps and shoulder-length blonde hair pulled back to reveal ears studded with small pearls.

"Ready, Jilly?" One of them called out. "Hey, Margo! Thanks for feeding Zanzibar for me the other day."

Margo smiled at the woman and wagged the crop in her direction.

"No problem, Portia," she said weakly. Her eyes returned to Jilly Travers' darkening face.

Portia mounted her dark bay gelding and flexed her gloved fingers against the reins.

"Jilly, I asked you if--"

"I heard you, Portia, darling," Jilly spat out, giving her horse's cavesson another unkind jerk. "I was just getting something straight with Margo here."

"What's the problem?" The other woman, Tess Andersen, spoke as she led her horse to where Margo and Jilly were standing.

"Well," Margo started, "I found this crop out in the eastern pasture--"

"*My* crop," Jilly hissed, turning her back on them to position her foot in her stirrup.

"Yes, well," Margo smiled hesitantly at Tess and Portia. "It's kind of messed up now.."

Jilly swung up into her saddle.

"It's been in the shit-hole for two weeks. I don't suppose you two know anything about it?" She stared at the two women.

Portia looked at the crop in Margo's hand. Tess jerked her head in Jilly's direction.

"What are you saying?" Tess asked. "You think one of us *stole* your crop?"

Jilly twisted the reins across her horse's neck and the animal turned away from the group. "What? *You* dear girls? What a thing to think." Jilly scowled at them from her saddle, her hands twitching against the reins.

"Oh, for heaven's sake." Tess swung up on her horse, stamping now in impatience. "What's the stupid thing cost? Twenty bucks?"

Portia twisted in her saddle and glared down at Margo.

"What's she saying? Is she saying *we* threw her crop in a pile of shit?"

"Forget it, Portia," Tess said. "She doesn't know *what* she's saying."

"I know more than you'd like me to know, darling Tess." Jilly's color seemed to fade a bit and another smile came to her lips. "I know that much."

"Look," Tess smacked a hand against her thigh. "Do you want to ride today, or not? Because I can do some ring work just as well. In fact, I probably *should*, so if you don't want--"

"On such a beautiful day? I would be heartbroken." Jilly smiled nastily then shook her head as Margo tried to hand her the crop. She held up a small child's bat and showed it to the barn manager. "I've got one, don't I, darling? It wouldn't make sense to ride with two, now, would it?"

"Don't be such a bitch, Jilly." Tess touched her horse's sides with her calves and she moved forward, away from the group. "You might end up ruining what should be a very pleasant hack."

2

Kathy Sue squinted at her notes and took a shallow breath and held it. The client had been very rude that morning, ruder even than usual. She flushed to remember the way he looked at her. Undressing her mentally and then casting her aside, untried. She reddened furiously and tried to read her shakily scribbled notes.

Her brief relief at not having to make the visit with Jilly was annihilated by the damage that Jilly had obviously performed on her visit to the man the day before.

Why does the bitch hate me? Kathy Sue wondered in hurt amazement. She reached nervously for her cigarettes and lit one up, watching the tip shake as she did so. No opportunity to humiliate her was left unexplored by Jilly Travers. And, as senior account executive, the opportunities were many.

Kathy Sue had been writing ad copy for Ryan, Davis and Shue for three years. Three years ago, she'd broken out of the in-house public relations department of a local hardware store chain, and made it to the big time: a real advertising agency. At first, the principals had loved her, treated her like family. Her then art director--an old geezer without an ounce of spite or competitiveness in his whole gangly, frail body--had helped train her in the business. The clients respected her, requested her presence at all the fact-finding meetings, and sent her nut and toffee baskets at Christmas. She had loved her job.

And then Jilly Travers came on board.

She came one year ago. With her saber-like painted talons, her waist-length dark hair, swinging provocatively as she moved down the halls, Jilly enticed clients and principals, junior art directors and portly media directors alike. She was beautiful and she was vicious. Her beauty was small and delicate. Her viciousness--considered an unexpected bonus in the business world of advertising--was rotund and deliberate.

Kathy Sue had good reasons to fear Jilly Travers. With Kathy Sue's plump figure, country-girl earnestness and eager smile, she was an irresistible target for derision. It was easy enough for Jilly to make Kathy Sue look incompetent in front of the principals. All she had to do was "forget" to give all the client information to Kathy Sue for a new ad, or perhaps to indulge in some ugly pillow-talk with *any one* of the three agency bosses.

Kathy Sue pushed her notes away and stared at her computer terminal. It had been months since anyone in the office had asked her to lunch or even dropped in to talk with her about anything besides work. She shifted in her chair and felt her plump thighs rub together uncomfortably.

Recently, Jilly hadn't been satisfied with merely orchestrating the destruction of Kathy Sue's career in-house. She had expanded her campaign to include the agency's client roster.

To one client, Jilly hinted that Kathy Sue was wildly promiscuous. Kathy Sue knew about the insinuations but felt powerless to defend herself to the client.

How to address it? And when? While they were all huddled around a new concept pitch? When they were in the boardroom enjoying a celebratory drink together?

Kathy Sue just didn't have the opportunities that Jilly did to speak privately to their clients. As a result, she sat, mortified and ashamed through meeting after meeting while the client watched her and leered. And while Jilly smiled. To another client--a man who had originally been fond of Kathy Sue as their copywriter--Jilly dropped the notion that Kathy Sue was lesbian and fiercely, if covertly, anti-male.

All in all, Kathy Sue had good reasons to fear Jilly Travers. And to hate her.

3

The sparrows skimmed the rafters, like the Blue Angels doing show-maneuvers, then settled in a flutter of brown and pale fluff around a pile of horse manure near the mouth of the lower barn.

Margo stood in the tacking-up area of the barn, watching the birds and filling in the creases of a leather halter with a lathering of saddle soap, rubbing it into the leather with firm strokes.

The afternoon darkened with threat of rain and she felt annoyed that the ride after her chores would probably not be possible. She found herself resenting the easy schedules most of her boarders enjoyed. If they weren't high-powered professionals with imminently flexible time tables, they were the non-working wives of high-powered professionals--with a limitless supply of beautiful mornings and sunny afternoons for riding or tennis or facials. She looked at the gleaming brass buckle on the halter she held. *And most of them didn't clean their own tack either.*

"Hey, Margo, check it out!"

Margo looked up from her work and blinked into the brightness as it pierced the stable entrance. She could discern the stark silhouette of someone approaching.

"What is it?" she called, her face frowning in the harsh light.

"Best-Boy just came back at a gallop without Travers."

The figure moved into the barn and suddenly her features developed before Margo's eyes. It was one of the pasture boarders. Elise or Elaine something. She had a mixed breed gelding in the west pasture that she didn't show or hunt but just sort of "pleasure rode." *Whatever that was.*

"What do you mean...'without Travers'?" Margo worked the soap into the halter a little harder.

The boarder approached and Margo could see that she held a green nylon halter. The girl was probably still in her teens.

"A couple of us are gonna go out and look for her. It'll take her an hour to walk back, *at least.* And it's gonna rain. Wanna come?"

"Where's Best-Boy now?" Margo knitted her eyebrows in a mask of concern. "Have you checked him out? Scratches or scrapes...?"

"Jessie caught him and threw him in the north paddock, tack and all." The girl shrugged her thin shoulders. She wore jeans and a sweatshirt with scuffed brown paddock boots. "Anyway, you coming? Jessie said we could bring Tucker for Jilly to ride back on."

"Look, I'm not sure this posse is really necessary. Jilly's with Portia Stephens and Tess Andersen. They ought--"

"Man, Margo, I thought Jessie told you. The girl began to retreat into the bright glare of the barn's entrance. "Portia and Tess came back forty minutes ago--"

"What?" Margo dropped the halter in the sawdust and then stooped to recover it.

"Yeah, Jessie said they told her they'd had a fight or something and left her out there."

"I see." Margo stared past the girl into the quickly dimming light of the afternoon outside. "And where are Portia and Tess now?" she asked.

The girl shrugged.

"I think Jessie said they went home already," she said. "Yeah, it'd been nice if they could help, huh?" She waved. "I'm tacking up Tucker, okay? We'll leave in five minutes if you want to come." She disappeared.

Margo held the leather halter tightly in her hands and stared after her.

4

The smell of the barn rose up from the straw-strewn floor: a combination of oily leather tack, manure, sweet feed and the sugary muskiness of the horses themselves.

Fulton County Senior Homicide Detective Jack Burton leaned against one of the stalls at the opening of the barn, having carefully avoided one of the ubiquitous brown piles that scattered the pathway, and surveyed the entire length of the barn with his flint-gray eyes. Fifteen box stalls on each side of the barn, most with long, curious noses poking out of them.

The Fulton County Police Department had gotten the call late that afternoon from someone at the Bon Chance Riding Stables in North Fulton County. Woman, presumed thrown from her horse on a ride in the woods, now missing. A search of the trail by the barn manager and a two others showed no sign of the woman but ample signs of a struggle. There was blood everywhere, on trees, rocks, the ground. The victim's blouse was found blood-sodden and rolled up under a rock, as if in a pathetic attempt to hide what could not possibly be hidden: someone had died there. Violently.

Now, hours later, in a gentle but quickly erasing rain, county forensics combed the area--ragged with tall pines, shrub and rocky trails-- while medics waited on-site in the relative warmth of their ambulance.

Burton watched a pair of barn sparrows bathe in a mud puddle by the barn's entrance. Black face, black bib...buffy breast, brown back stripes. Pine Woods sparrows, he wondered? Aren't they a little too far south? He listened to the soft nickering of the horses in their stalls as they munched noisily on the remnants of their dinners. As he listened to the horses eat and watched the sparrows, he wondered if he were feeling a little saved or a little mad.

"Noisy little buggers, aren't they?"

Jack's back stiffened. Lately, his partner, David Kazmaroff, had taken to sprinkling English expressions in his usually thickly Southern-accented dialogue. Burton had been convinced he did it solely to annoy him, but it *was* possible, he supposed, that Kazmaroff had begun the habit as a result of his bizarre attempt to become the last bonafide, living Yuppie of the nineties.

Just when everyone else wants to bury their BMWs and pasta makers and start cleaning up the environment, this moron wants to interrogate child molesters using an English accent.

Dave Kazmaroff had jumped at the chance to work on this case, Burton knew. Bon Chance Farm was the headquarters of the Atlanta Polo Club. Burton knew that if there was anything Kazmaroff, with his Ralph Lauren shirts and Armani jackets, wanted most to be associated with --it was "the sport of Kings."

"Okay, so who's on our list?" Burton sighed heavily, his pleasure in the barn spoiled by his partner's presence.

Kazmaroff shifted his weight and leaned against the stall next to Burton. He flipped open his notebook, his brow puckered in concentration.

"The barn manager lives on the property," he said. "A Margo Sherman. She's the one who called the police and did the first search. Surprised she's not here to meet us."

"Who else?"

"Well, there's the two girls who had the fight and left her out there. They don't live here, of course."

"Of course." Burton turned back toward the dozing horses in their stalls. "Who else lives on the property?" he asked.

Dave checked his small spiral notebook again.

"The manager, Margo, a stable groom, name of Jessie Parker, and a grounds man..."

"Grounds man?" Burton looked back at Kazmaroff. "You mean, like a gardener?"

Kazmaroff smiled thinly at his partner, showing big, straight teeth.

"I imagine he tends the polo fields," he said pleasantly. "Name's Bill Lint." He snapped the notebook shut with a quick flip of his wrist and the horse in the stall nearest to him started abruptly, its eyes white and wide for a moment before relaxing again. "That's all I know," he said, unaware of the animal's reaction.

Burton turned away again to hide his agitation while taking refuge in the sounds of the big, sleepy beasts tucked into their stalls for the night.

"Well," he said tightly. "Then let's find Miss Sherman, shall we?" He turned to make his way out of the warm barn when a figure emerged from the barn's tack room and storage area.

"That won't be necessary," a husky voice said. "I'm Margo Sherman." The woman was big, Burton noted. And quiet. He wondered how long she had been in the tack room listening.

"Blimey! You startled me," Dave said as he slapped a meaty hand to his heart and grinned at her.

It was all Burton could do not to imbed a stiff right in the man's solar plexus.

Blimey?

Instead, he concentrated on the woman.

"Detective Jack Burton," he said, showing his I.D. "This is my partner, Detective Kazmaroff."

She nodded at both of them and rubbed her hands across the thighs of her no-longer clean riding breeches.

"I've got an office here," she said. "We could talk there."

Burton smiled professionally at her.

"Lead on," he said.

Margo Sherman sat opposite the detectives in her cramped office, crowded by towering horse show trophies, clumps of multi-colored prize ribbons that draped the walls, and a couple of saddles perched on wooden saddle rests. Her desk was an untidy pile of vet bills, farrier notes and equine medical manuals. The place smelled of leather and sweet grain and Burton found himself quite comfortable in the setting.

Margo stirred up three cups of instant coffee in chipped and broken-handled mugs, then sat waiting for the detectives' questions.

"I can't believe this is happening," she said, pushing a shock of her long brown hair from her too-tan face. "I mean, Jilly's a good rider, you know? And Best-Boy--that's her horse--Best-Boy..." She looked helplessly at the two detectives. "...is such a good horse," she finished lamely.

Kazmaroff opened his notebook and bent his leg up over his knee. He leaned forward and Burton could see the impression of a medallion of some kind under his knit shirt. The only thing he lacks for oiliness, Burton thought, trying not to look at him, was a gold tooth.

"Is Mrs. Travers married?" Kazmaroff asked.

"Uh, she was." Margo's eyes flitted to a framed picture on the wall of a line of horses and riders, obviously taken at some horse show. "She's divorced. Has a son," she added.

Kazmaroff cocked an eyebrow.

Margo bit her lip.

"This is really unbelievable," she said. "I can't imagine where she...what could've happened to her." She looked at Burton. "Do you think she's dead?"

He watched her eyes.

"It doesn't look good," he said. "How old is her son?"

"Oh, he doesn't live with her." She picked up her cooling coffee and took a sip. "He's, like, eighteen or something. And they weren't very close."

"Oh?" Kazmaroff encouraged her with a smile.

"I mean, I got the *impression* that they weren't, you know?" She spoke hurriedly, putting her coffee down on the desk. "I mean, Jilly complained about him a lot, you know? Like they weren't..." She looked unhappily at Burton. "...weren't very close."

"What can you tell us about the two women who rode out with Ms. Travers?" Burton asked. His smile seemed frozen in place now.

She took a big breath. This was obviously the question she had been waiting for.

"Tess Andersen and Portia Stephens," she said. "They're, like, best friends, right? Always out here together."

"Friends of Jilly Travers?" Kazmaroff asked.

Margo licked her lips and glanced again at the photo over her desk. Burton noticed.

"Well, I guess," she said slowly. "I don't know. They were always kind of sniping at each other, you know?"

"Sniping?" Burton prompted.

"Well, not so much Portia. She's pretty easy to get along with. I guess mostly just Jilly and Tess. I'm not sure why they rode together so much."

"But they did?"

"Oh, yes, quite a lot." Margo took a big breath. "Do you think they had anything to do with this?"

"What do you think, Miss Sherman?"

"God, I don't know what to think." Her lips trembled and Burton thought she might be on the verge of an emotional outburst but she seemed to restrain herself. "I like Tess a lot. I suppose I consider her a friend of sorts."

"Of sorts."

"Well, I mean, I do work here and all. It's not like we live in the same circle. But when she's here she always treats me..." Margo looked as if she wished she hadn't begun this line of thought. "...you know, quite well."

"Not like the hired help, in other words?" Kazmaroff's voice boomed out jovially and Burton found himself surprised and grateful for his partner's open and cheery slamming of the hammer on the nail's head.

"That's pretty...pretty rude, isn't it?" she said, looking at Burton in dismay as if asking for his support. "I do a job here, that's right." Her face flushed darkly. "That doesn't make me some dirty stable hand or something...I...my relationship with Tess is based on..." She looked around her office as if looking for the words among her trophies. "...on mutual respect. She doesn't fly in here and ask me to fetch her horse from the pasture for her or mend her tack or deal with the farrier for her. I mean, she respects the value of my time."

"But you do muck out her horse's stall?" Burton asked.

"I don't, personally, no," she responded hotly.

"Did Jilly Travers ask you to do things for her?" Burton touched one of the trophies on the shelf nearest to him. It had been dusted recently.

"From time to time." Margo wrung her hands. "That's not unusual, you know. Most of the boarders...some of them need things and I *am* the barn manager."

"Lot of great trophies you got here." Kazmaroff stood up and swept his hand in a wide arc at them all. "You win all these?"

Margo nodded.

"Did people like Mrs. Travers?" he asked her as he held a trophy up to his face and squinted to read the inscription.

"Fairly well," she said, watching him.

"Did you like her?"

"Well enough. Look, am I suspect or something?" Her voice had become shrill and she was now wringing her long fingers in front of her.

Burton exchanged a look with Kazmaroff, amazed at the lack of friction he normally felt with him during a questioning.

"We're just collecting information, Miss Sherman," Burton said quietly moving to his feet. "It's not pleasant, but it does take awhile, I'm afraid. We'll probably have to spend some time here."

Margo nodded and stole another glance at the picture across from her desk. She looked totally miserable.

"Of course," she said.

5

The clearing was not large. It huddled in the center of a group of spindly but towering Georgia pines. A mass of grass and weeds, twitching in the softly falling rain, sat in forlorn bunches along the perimeter marking the borders of the crime scene.

Burton and Kazmaroff parked their car alongside the coroner's wagon, three police cruisers, and two dark-colored vans, belonging to the photographer and forensic specialists.

Kazmaroff tossed a cigarette butt into the night as they stepped out of the car. A tall, barrel-chested man with sandy-blond hair and pale green eyes, he was considered by most women to be good looking, and downright hunk material by the precinct's secretaries. A faint, jagged scar across his right eyebrow did little to diminish the assessment.

He pointed at the mess of muddy tire tracks around them.

"You're not thinking what I'm thinking, are you?" he asked in a disgusted grunt.

Burton noted the tracks and shook his head. "They wouldn't be so stupid." He looked up at the darkening sky and flipped his collar back against the light rain which ran like cold flecks of rice down his neck. "God, I hope they wouldn't be so stupid."

They entered the clearing, the opening in the dense brush surrounding it had been hacked considerably wider since the first police cruiser had been called to the scene nearly six hours ago.

"Jesus! Is there anything they didn't drive over, park on, or rip through? Who was first on the scene?" Kazmaroff said in disgust.

Burton slid a little in the dense mud as he trudged ahead of Kazmaroff. A hundred yards away, he heard the burping of police radios and the drift of voices on the wind.

Beyond the perimeter of yellow banner guard tape corralling the clearing, a makeshift tent had been pitched against the drizzle. In the fading light, Burton could make out the standing silhouette of Jim Merritt, the medical examiner. Not much to do without a body, Burton thought grimly as he and Kazmaroff approached. Two uniformed officers stood outside the tent while a photographer set up his camera for pictures of every angle of the scene. A fifth man emerged from a wall of honeysuckle and jasmine bushes clutching a video camera. Both photographers were draped in county-issue ponchos.

A mild scent of iron fillings and wet fur filled Burton's nostrils and he steeled himself not to hold his breath. The whole point, he reminded himself, was to experience it all, notice it all.

"Smells like a massacre's worth of blood," Kazmaroff said, sniffing, still struggling up the slippery path behind Burton. "Smells like half a platoon died here."

More Iraqi war references. Did he never let up?

The two detectives stopped at the tent opening where Merritt waited with the two police officers. Without bothering to greet them, Burton jerked his head toward the path they'd just left.

"Which one of you guys was the first on the scene this afternoon?" He knew his admonishment was going to sound limp--after all, this was the *second* visit he and Kazmaroff had made to the crime scene.

"Frikens, sir," the youngest-looking cop said and stiffened as he did so, almost coming to attention. He was fair and pink-faced. Burton softened a little.

"And where is Frikens?" Kazmaroff wiped the rain from his face and ducked under the eaves of the tent.

"He had to leave." The man's eyes never left Burton.

He may be green but he knows which superior to keep his eyes on.

"Did anyone check tire tracks off the main road into this place?" he asked with a sigh.

"Tire tracks?"

"Yeah, you know, on the ground we're all using for a parking lot? Tire tracks?"

The young cop swallowed and allowed his eyes to flicker toward the direction where he knew the police cars and vans were parked.

"I...I'm not sure, sir."

The weariness came back to Burton and he gently pushed past the man. "Check it out," he said as he entered the tent.

Kazmaroff and the medical examiner followed him inside. Burton walked to a small table stacked with styrofoam cups and two large thermoses of coffee. He poured himself a cup. He didn't offer to do the same for Kazmaroff, who waited patiently to pour his own.

Jim Merritt, the medical examiner, blocked the opening of the tent with his body. He was a large man, tall and fat, his bulk quivering under his thin polo shirt. His eyes were sharp but kind, and his upper lip stuck out over the bottom lip, reminding Burton of a petulant bird's beak. Jim was a jovial soul, good at what he did, and generally pleasant to have around.

“Where’s the police agent?” Burton asked. “What’s his name?”

“Darwin,” Merritt answered. “He’s out there somewhere. They've combed for the last six hours," he said. "Still nothing."

"Have they stopped for the day?" Burton turned with his steaming cup, and squinted in the man's direction.

"It's raining, Jack," Merritt said. "*Been* raining for nearly an hour now. It won't stop any time soon."

"What did we get?" Kazmaroff spoke over his shoulder as he tipped the coffee into his cup, its fragrance mercifully blotting out the stale air of the tent.

Merritt shrugged and half turned to open the tent flap and peer out.

"Lots of blood," he said. "We should at least be able to match it to the alleged victim's blood-type."

"But...?" Kazmaroff prompted.

"Would help to have a body," Merritt said turning back to face Kazmaroff. "Or something." He shrugged. "Teeth, hair, a body limb..."

"Anything else?" Burton interrupted.

"Darwin checked the bushes, twigs, kindling, insects, scratches on trees, depressed areas in the grass--seems the clearing also serves as a deer bedding ground--we found some animal spoor and tiny bones..."

"And there's nothing." Burton said. He took a long sip of his coffee and stared out the opening into the darkening landscape. A pair of juncos seemed to stare down at him from the limb of an ancient magnolia tree. They tittered briefly.

"Oh, there's a lot of blood," Merritt said softly. "There's blood on the ground, on the bushes, on a tree or two. One of my men found a few drops in her horse's hair."

"How about an escape route?" Kazmaroff's voice seemed to boom out and suck up all the air in the tent. Burton began to feel too warm. "Figure out how the bastard got away?"

Merritt shrugged.

"The assumption at this point is that he left the way he came."

"Which was?"

"Probably from the road." Merritt nodded toward the path the two detectives had just walked up. "But you'll need to talk to Darwin about that." He smiled. "Or better yet, officers, check it out yourselves. It's a very tight circle of shrubbery and trees. He'd have to be half rabbit to have come any other way."

"Barn manager says riders come through this trail all the time."

"There's no evidence the guy was on horseback."

"No evidence he wasn't," Kazmaroff said smugly.

"You gotta scenario, Dave?" Burton said, turning to his partner.

"Yeah, okay," Kazmaroff said, puffing his chest out an inch. "How about this? How about the three girls fight, one of 'em or both of 'em kills the Travers girl..."

"From horseback?" Burton sipped his coffee and glanced at Merritt's slowly grinning face as they both listened.

"Okay, they got off their horses. Okay? On their horses, off their horses...the point is..."

"Jesus, Dave, the point is, how did they dispose of the body if they're all on horseback?" Burton shook his head and turned back to the medical examiner.

"I'm just saying, there's more than one way outta this clearing," Kazmaroff said, frowning.

"That's true," Burton said. He nodded as he spoke and tossed his empty cup into a paper bag. "But nobody heard a helicopter land and we've found no evidence of a tunnel, so I'm afraid we're--"

"Oh, give it a rest, man." The fury in Kazmaroff's voice was real and it was sudden.

"Let's all give it a rest," Merritt said, trying to gloss over the moment between the two men. "It's been a long hard afternoon and it looks like it's all coming to nothing." He waved a hand at the falling rain.

Burton avoided looking at Kazmaroff, concentrating, instead, on watching the rain as if the body might somehow be hidden up in the branches of the trees. "What about the dogs?" he asked calmly. "When are they coming?"

Merritt shrugged and Burton turned his body a few inches towards Kazmaroff.

"The guy said he'd get here as soon as he could," Kazmaroff said. "Tonight, some time."

"All this blood...the murder weapon has to be a knife, or a pick-axe or something, right?" he said to no one in particular.

"My guess is a very large knife."

The voice was attached to a slim African-American male who spoke as he pushed the flap back on the tent.

"Gus Darwin," he said, shaking hands with both detectives. "We haven't found anything yet but obviously some major arteries or veins were cut." He turned again to survey the clearing, thick with cloudy shadows.

"Any sign of the body being dragged away?" Burton asked.

"No, and that's really strange, you know?" Darwin said. "No dragging marks, no blood leading off to someplace. The path to the road? Not a drop, not a hair."

"That you could find," Kazmaroff said.

Burton looked at Kazmaroff and gave him a sour look.

"That is correct, Detective Kazmaroff," Darwin said cheerfully. "Any coffee left? And although it's true that, technically, my job involves collecting and recording evidence of the site and the corpus, as it were--which investigating officers have not yet provided for me," he said, smiling pointedly at Kazmaroff, "I did while away some time here this pleasant afternoon helping out the
searchers--"

"Look, man, I'm sorry, I--"

"--and I must report that, you're right, there was no trace of body or murder weapon to be found." He paused. "Except for, of course, the footprint."

Burton and Kazmaroff both looked up at once.

"I didn't mention the footprint?" Darwin smiled enigmatically. "There were several, of course, there would have to be, wouldn't there?" He moved outside and they followed. The rain was harder now coming down in a gentle but insistent flow.

"There'd been an attempt to obfuscate," Darwin continued. “See? It looks too deliberate, all this scraping...like it was done with the side of a boot or something." He pointed to a small cordoned off area on the ground, now only recognizable as a four foot by five foot patch of mud. "So I guess you guys will be determining whether or not this indicates if there had been a struggle, or not. There are really no direct signs leading to it..."

"But you got a print?" Kazmaroff interrupted, spilling his coffee on his hand as he attempted to pull his shirt collar against the rain.

"Quite a good one, actually," Darwin said happily. "I'll transport the cast back to the lab to have a shoe track made of it." He shrugged. "It's something," he said.

Burton watched the photographers wrap up their expensive equipment and hurry down the pathway to their waiting vans. He and Kazmaroff would need to coordinate with them later on, pick up the finished prints, cart the forty or so paper boxes of twigs and blood-splotched leaves and dirt clods back to the police lab, send a sketcher back out at first light. Had Kazmaroff gotten the names of all the boarders? He glanced at his watch. A little after seven and they still had to visit Jilly Traver's condo tonight.

"It's great," he said absently. "A print is really great."

Normally, he knew, the first twenty-four hours in a case were the most critical in establishing clues and identifying physical evidence. He looked at the scene around him and watched the grass and bushes as they turned into black murky shadows in the downpour. Then, he turned, with the others, to the protection of the tent.

Chapter Two

1

"If you're going to sit that pony like a comatose jellyfish, I'm not going to waste a minute further of my time with you!"

Margo strode over to the quivering child atop a Welsh pony and clapped her hands together smartly.

"Now, wake *up*, Haley!"

"I'm trying, Miss Margo," the child whimpered, the tendrils of her auburn hair escaping her bulky black velvet hard-hat.

Margo patted the pony's neck and felt suddenly overwhelmed by the lesson, the heat, the interaction with the child. She nodded.

"I know you are, dear," she said, patting the child's booted leg now. "Let's try again next week, shall we? Do you want to ride around the ring or are you ready to untack?"

"I want to go home." The girl's pretty face looked like a cloud of waiting tears and Margo felt instantly sickened by her own behavior.

God, I'm starting to act like Jilly.

"All right, darling," she said, taking the pony's reins. "Hop down, then. I'll take care of Dancer." She watched the girl scramble off the animal and run, without looking back, to her mother and their waiting Mercedes sports vehicle. Margo waved feebly at the woman, who squinted at her through dark sunglasses.

I can kiss that fifty bucks a week good-bye, she thought, as she watched the mother remove the girl's riding hat and smooth back her damp curls. The child talked with animation to her concerned parent.

Margo led the pony back to the barn and tugged off the small English saddle. She looked down the row of horses' stalls to see if she could see or hear Jessie but she was alone.

She plopped the saddle down on a nearby saddle rack and retrieved the pony's halter from the tack room. It helped to work, to keep moving, keep busy. Looking for Jessie to untack the pony so she could go back to her office and mope was hardly wise psychological management, she told herself sternly.

She removed Dancer's bridle, hooking it on a nearby nail, and snaked his worn leather halter over his nose and ears. She buckled the throat latch and then tied him to a ring in front of one of the stalls.

If only she could stop thinking about everything: Jilly. Tess. If only she could just go about her work and take each day as it came. And whatever came, she would handle it. Her ears strained to hear the sound of the phone ringing. Nothing.

She picked up each of the pony's little feet, cleaned out his shoes, and painted the frogs and soles with a thrush prophylactic. With the recent heavy rains, she knew the horses would all be more prone to developing fungus.

She straightened up from her work and looked down the middle of the barn again. What was she looking for? Was it Jessie? Or did she expect those detectives to come back? One of the boarders said they had had to practically drive in a ditch this morning to get past all the cop cars and vans along the side of the road. They must have returned early. Bill had already reported to her that they'd left at least one man on guard in the clearing all night. She wondered if that was standard procedure.

Did they expect the killer to come back?

She picked up a large dandy brush and cleaned away the sweat from the pony's saddle area. He'd not had much of a work-out this morning, so she just brushed him lightly, groomed his mane and tail, then wiped out his eyes. The pony belonged to the barn and was used for lessons and, occasionally hired out as a trail horse. He looked up at her with large, slowly blinking eyes, like glassy pools of darkness. She felt a ridiculous urge to hug the animal and that surprised her. She hadn't felt such a sensation since she'd been a horse-crazy youngster. Just about Haley's age. A pang of guilt pierced her. She turned and led the pony to its stall.

Back in her office, she peeled off her calf-length chaps and tossed them in a cracked leather-look swivel chair in the corner, then heaved herself into her desk chair.

What had they thought of her? Did they think she might have killed Jilly?

The young detective was cute in a kind of boring, generic way, she thought. But the other one, Burton, had a kind of particularity to his looks. Dark, tousled hair...
wasn't the police department all supposed to have super short hair? and those blue-blue eyes. Altogether very rugged-looking, she decided. In a messy, just rolled out of the sack kind of way. And very dishy.

Margo loosened her belt two notches. She was a large woman, made up of sharp angles and soft spots, she was a physical contradiction in many ways. She caught a shadow of her reflection in the glass of the large group photo on the wall opposite her desk. Her jaw sprang out in Germanic insistency, yet her face was yielding and vulnerable. Was it the eyes? She blinked away her own image and stared directly at the photograph. Three men, four women, in complete fox- hunting regalia. Jilly, looking smug and mean, her long black hair caught up in a tight net and screwed to the back of her pale, long neck. Next to her was her then-husband, Mark Travers, looking somehow defenseless next to his wife. His smile was genuine and broad. His eyes laughed at the photographer. They hadn't been married very long, Margo thought grimly. And then there was Tess Andersen. Beautiful, blonde, and cool. As dangerous, in her way, as Jilly, Margo noted. Tess stood at the edge of the group. Uncoupled, unattached. Her eyes looked clear and penetrating, her smile, false. Next to her, Portia Stephens hugged her arms in her snug dark riding coat, her crop held up against her face like a threat. Her face was open and vacant. Pretty, Margo thought with surprise. It wasn't usually the first thing one noticed about Portia. Normally, it was the flat, dead eyes. The doors to the vacant house. Portia's husband stood next to her, uncomfortable and awkward in his riding pinks. He had a broad face with too-rosy cheeks and lips. His eyes were small and piggy, Margo thought. He wasn't a horseman. He was an outsider. He looked it, he rode it, and he photographed it. Margo dismissed him, and then looked at the photograph of herself. A younger...*when was this picture taken? Ten years ago? Fifteen?*...more eager version of herself. Slimmer too, she noted tiredly. Her own riding partner stood rigidly beside her. Todd something or other. She hadn't known him very well, never dated him again, and only agreed to ride with him for the hunt because she felt out-numbered by the Travers and Stephens. Tess didn't need to have a date. She was beautiful and, well, Tess. Margo had felt in need of the crutch. Later, Margo always felt a tinge of vexation that the man had been included in the group shot. She looked at the whole picture again. So young, so full of fire and good times. She was a trainer then, not a barn manager. And although she couldn't keep up with her friends financially, she was the better equestrienne, and felt respected and accepted by them. Her eyes scanned the black and white photo. So young, she thought.

Her eyes fell on the laughing face of Jilly's ex-husband. A month after the picture was taken, she and Mark Travers had begun their affair.

2

It was a little before six in the morning. The night had been cold for November in Georgia and the morning was foggy and gray. Burton stepped into Jilly Travers' West Paces Ferry condominium, carefully placing the keys in his jacket pocket and moving aside to let Kazmaroff enter behind him. Instantly, he was struck by an almost palpable feeling of evil in the hallway. It was like a bad smell, except that there was no fragrance, no real scent of any kind in the place. Shaking off the feeling, Burton concentrated on taking a mental inventory of the apartment. Kazmaroff, he knew, would be taking notes. Burton preferred to work with initial impressions and feelings coupled with whatever facts were available. As far as he was concerned, when it came right down to it, a detective's instincts were all that separated him from the uniforms guarding the apartment door out front.

From the hallway, he and Kaz emerged into the condo's living room, everything appeared as cold and austere as the light in her eyes from every photo of her he'd ever seen. He walked through the living room and the small den. There were no signs of her riding hobby, no family pictures, no trophies from work or the riding ring, no indication that the kitchen was used for anything other than heating up the occasional cup of coffee.

Her bedroom was equally cold and forbidding. Done in stark whites and grays, it looked as unused as the gleaming, stainless steel kitchen. Burton found himself impressed with its spartan decor. His own wife, if she had her way, would wallpaper their entire three bedroom bungalow in cabbage roses and vining violets. A reeking net-ball of potpourri was always tumbling out at him from some drawer, closet, or shelf. Kazmaroff, on the other hand, was appalled.

"Jesus! Did she sleep here at night or just hang upside down in the closet?"

"Different tastes," Burton muttered, annoyed that they were, once again, on polar opposite wavelengths.

Jilly's closet, however, was packed with designer color. Burton bit back all comment as his partner reeled off the names of each designer as if they hung inside his own closet too.

"Donna Karan, YSL, Blass, Dolce & Gabbana...this chick liked to dress nice."

Was he trying to get a rise out of him? Was he trying to see if Burton would affect to know the names too?

Burton ignored him and headed toward the fragile-looking antique desk next to Jilly's bed.

He rifled through a few bill stubs for water and cable. The woman seemed to have paid everything promptly, as soon as it came in. Burton thought this odd. People as hard-nosed in business as Jilly supposedly was, didn't pay their bills as soon as they came in, but waited until just before they were due, so their own banking accounts could retain every penny of interest due them. Why let creditors have one day more than necessary of compounding interest? He put his hand on Jilly's engagement calendar, surprised to find it here and not at her office. Unless she was a control freak, he thought. Then she wouldn't be able to help herself paying the bills as they came in. The feeling of wanting that clean slate would be too overwhelming. He flipped to the present week and found the date on which she disappeared. On it, she'd scrawled: *barn*. And then, *call Shue at home*.

"Find anything?" Kazmaroff, obviously tired of showing off his Women's Weekly expertise when noone was listening, peered over Burton's shoulder.

Burton straightened up and snapped the diary shut. He was about to pop it into one of the paper bags they'd brought for evidence when the note fluttered to the soft, gray carpeting.

Kazmaroff was quicker than he. He snatched it up and opened the four-folded sheet. "Christ, it's a blackmail note," he said.

Burton grabbed it from him. It read, in innocuous serif type: *I'll make you sorry. I'll make you dead sorry someday.*

"Now, the real question is," Kazmaroff said with a self-satisfied smile as he leaned against one of her stark bedroom walls. "Is this little missive *to* Miss Jilly? Or *from* her?"

Burton pressed his right foot into the floorboard of the Ford's passenger seat. He hated it when Kazmaroff drove. Fact is, he hated it when anyone drove but himself. He eased off the imaginary brake pedal and forced himself to relax into the dark upholstery. The scenery flew by in a panorama of brown and mossy-green countryside. He flipped open Kazmaroff's notebook and tightened his face into a knot of effort.

"I can't read this shit," he said over the hum of the engine. "Something about...a ball of lint...?"

"Bill Lint," Kazmaroff said, snapping on his right turn signal. "The groundskeeper at the farm. He's got a trailer near the murder site."

"*You* should be reading this," Burton said. "It's *your* handwriting. And thanks for the bombshell," he said sarcastically. "Our guys go through it?"

Kazmaroff nodded, unaffected by his partner's tone.

"Place was clean."

"Besides, he's got an airtight."

"Yeah, the barn manager said he was with her that afternoon."

"Convenient." Burton tossed the notebook onto the dashboard.

"Maybe, yes, maybe, no," Kazmaroff said, turning off Georgia 400 onto State Highway 121 and heading east. "The stable girl, Jessie? Said Lint, like, adored Jilly Travers."

Burton grunted and motioned to an upcoming convenience store. "Pull over and let me grab a paper," he said.

Kazmaroff turned into the parking lot and parked the cruiser in front of the store. He turned off the engine but Burton made no move to get out.

"So what've we got so far?" Burton asked, his eyes staring through the windshield as if talking to himself.

Kazmaroff shifted his weight and unhooked his seatbelt.

"Well," he said slowly. "We got a dead woman--"

"Presumed dead," Burton corrected.

"Yeah, okay, fine." Kazmaroff rolled his eyes. "We got a maybe dead woman. A blood-saturated area of about twenty feet by fifteen. An illiterate gardener with no motive and no opportunity. A foot print--which could be the victim's footprint for all we know. And a couple of weak tread prints from a car other than the circus ground of tire prints Atlanta's finest created. We got shit."

"Don't forget the blackmail note," Burton said, finally turning to look at his partner.

"Oh, yeah." Dave shrugged and looked out the window. Although technically part of Atlanta, this section of Highway 121 was still in the country. The lone convenience store stood out against a backdrop of virgin timber and thick scrub. A line of ten public telephones huddled against the front wall of the store. Burton noticed a pair of mourning doves settled on top of one of the phone boxes. He wondered if they were waiting around for hand-outs.

"So far, I'm trying to find somebody who couldn't have written it." He looked back at Burton. "She didn't seem to have been exactly lovable."

Burton paid for his morning edition of the Atlanta Journal/Constitution and a small carton of dusty-white doughnuts Kazmaroff had insisted he pick up for him. Through the window of the convenience store, he could see Kazmaroff talking on his cell phone, and he felt a pang of dismay. He hated it when the bastard got the juicy bits first. He inevitably tried to feed them to Burton from a string attached to a stick--like a farmer and his addled coon dog. The thought of it made Burton move toward the door before the cashier had finished counting out all his change. Tempted to tell the smiling Pakistani to keep it and loathe to give away nearly four bucks, Burton took a deep breath and returned to the counter. He could already hear Kazmaroff's affected, deep voice: "Guess what, partner?" No, that was a little too friendly for Kazmaroff at this stage of the game. He might've been foolish enough to have addressed Burton like that last year. No such mistake would be made today.

Burton swung open his car door and tossed the doughnuts to Kazmaroff. He'd be damned if he'd ask the jerk what he found out.

"HQ says Jilly's ex-husband, Mark Travers, has an alibi for the day in question, but that he will be, and I quote, more than happy to speak with us at our convenience."

Burton felt his body sag a bit with relief. *That was all?*

"So we can put him off a bit, huh?" Kazmaroff pushed two of the miniature doughnuts into his mouth, spilling a tiny clot of powdered sugar down the front of his wine-colored polo shirt.

The pleasure of the ruined shirt softened Burton' irritation. "He'll wait," Burton said. "On to the Portia Stephens' portion of our program," he said lightly. "Are we pretty close?"

"Oh yeah, hey, one other thing," Kazmaroff said as he started the engine. "You know that footprint? Turns out there must've been more than just horses and three girls prancing around in that clearing." He smiled at Burton deliberately. "Lab says the print belonged to a male, approximately six feet, one hundred and ninety pounds. Hey, man, you want to drive?"

3

Portia smoothed out the silky folds of her mid-calf skort and stood a foot back from the French doors that opened onto the widow's walk. Her friends had thought it silly--Jilly and Tess specifically--to build a walk with no hope of water for four hundred miles. But she had insisted on having it built. Since she was a little girl in Savannah, she'd wanted one, had wanted the feel of standing on one, the ache in her eyes of watching for her returning sailor. Now that she was grown, she wouldn't let a thing like living in the middle of a country park or the fact that her returning sailor was really a slightly pudgy attorney who returned every night from his law office in a cherry red Lexus convertible stop her from having her widow's walk. Six months ago, her house had been featured in Southern Homes and Living, but the widow's walk--the best part of the whole house--had not been photographed or mentioned. She told herself she didn't care. Like her Gramma Rose used to say: what other people felt or thought didn't matter a drop. Not a drop in the bucket.

From her vantage point, she watched the approaching police cruiser wind its way along the curving driveway. She watched it slowly take the ambling switch backs, past the sentinels of azaleas and dogwood, the towering beech and willows. She wondered if they thought the grounds were beautiful. It was late autumn and everything was past its glory point, but still remarkable.

She touched the pearls against her throat as she momentarily lost sight of the police car behind a stand of towering sycamores. She absently caressed the pearls, enjoying their warmth, the warmth they stole from her own skin.

"You remember, darling? What we talked about? The fight?"

"You mean I can tell them about the fight?"

"Of course, tell them about the fight. Portia, darling, what part don't you understand?"

"I wish you were going to be here, Tess."

"Portia, it's very simple. Just tell them what happened. And then stop."

"What if they ask what happened after we left Jilly?"

"They want to know what happened in the clearing, dear. Not how we made our way back to the barn. They won't ask."

"But what if they do?"

Portia's eyes followed the police cruiser as it rounded the last stand of camouflaging trees and broke into the clearing that presented the main house. Her ears still hummed with the words from Tess' early morning phone call:

"Do not tell them what happened after we left the clearing. Do you hear me, Portia? Do not tell them what happened once we left."

4

Kathy Sue's hands trembled as she picked up the manila folder and nodded at Bob Shue. Business as usual. Get the product catalog put together for tomorrow's meeting. Rough layouts were fine but finished copy was expected. She wore a mask of concentrated attentiveness but every fiber in her wanted to explode, to sing, to run screaming and shrieking through the sedate advertising offices, to do a series of backflips across the conference room table, watching the crystal and brass figurine awards bobble and shake in her wake.

Missing, presumed dead.

As in, not coming back to work. Not today, not ever. The solemn announcement was made at the traffic meeting as if it were just another--albeit quite serious--scheduling problem to be unsnarled, and then on with tracking catalogs and brochures and ads and media deadlines. Kathy Sue wanted to risk a glance at her boss, Robert Shue, but didn't dare.

Carrying her load of manila folders and product fabric swatches for the shop-at-home client they'd just signed, she hurried back to her cubby-hole office, passing Jilly's large cavern of an office as she went. A yellow ribbon sealed off the door. Police Line. Do Not Cross. Kathy Sue slowed and peered through the glassed walls. A young, unsmiling policewoman stood inside looking through Jilly's filing cabinet. Kathy Sue felt a thrill run through her and continued her way to her own office. It's true. It's really true. The bitch is dead.

"Yo, K.S!"

Kathy Sue whirled around, nearly dropping her load of papers, to face a young, scraggly-bearded art director coming up from behind. Alex Wimmers. He was talented, new to the group, and up to this moment, quite standoffish. Kathy Sue stared at him and frowned. He was in the meeting. He knew his deadline. What was his problem?

"Bunch of us heading out to an early lunch, talk about what went down with Jilly. Wanna come?" He smiled at her. Kathy Sue stared at him.

"Yo!" the artist said. "Lunch. You. Me. Others. Yes?" The smile stayed put.

Kathy Sue nodded, a smile trying to form on her face.

"Yeah, okay," she said slowly.

"We'll come get you." He shook his head and walked away. "Wake up, honey. It's all gonna start happening now."

Kathy Sue knew he meant the workload, knew he was referring to the extra scramble that would result from losing their top account executive with nobody suitable to handle her clients. But she felt something else by his words. She felt something wonderful and releasing and good.

It's all gonna start happening now.

She went into her office and closed the door to call Ned, her fiancé, to tell him she wouldn't be coming home in tears anymore, wouldn't have to drink half a bottle of cooking sherry just to get some sleep, wouldn't have to take those pills to keep her stomach from hopping, her ears from ringing.

The bitch was dead and it was all gonna start happening now.

5

Margo looked at her hand as it dialed the phone. Dirt was caked under the nails, her knuckles were grimy and lined. The older she got, the harder she seemed to be working. Was that the way it was supposed to be? She waited while the line rang on the other end. Be casual, she said to herself. Be cool.

"Hello?" The voice on the other line sounded guarded but there was a lilt to it as if to affect indifference.

"Tess? It's Margo."

"Yes?"

Margo's heart sank.

"I...I thought you might have called me," she said, her voice heavy with disappointment. "That maybe I missed your call--"

"I didn't call, Margo," Tess said. "Why? Is Wizard okay? Has something happened?"

"Wizard...?" For a moment, Margo had no idea of who or what Tess was talking about.

"You know, the thing I ride on when I come to the barn? My horse?"

"Jesus, Tess! What is your problem?" Margo didn't know what to say to her. It was obvious Tess wasn't feeling like commiserating. "I just called to see if you were...if you were okay--"

"If I were okay?" Tess's voice sounded supercilious, and piercingly condescending. Margo was horrified for having dialed the phone.

"After...after what happened..." she muttered. "I just thought...the police have been here all day yesterday and all morning..."

"Look, Margo, maybe it's a good thing you called."

Margo took a huge breath and tried to steady her nerves.

We used to be friends, didn't we? Riding pals? Friends?

"I can't come out to ride" Tess continued. "But I know the farrier's coming today. Could you make sure that Wizard isn't turned out? He's a bitch to catch in the pasture, you know, and Joe's complained about it before. Is that a problem?"

Margo hung up on the cool, pleasant voice, and tried to take another long breath. *Screw you, Tess*, she thought.

Screw the hell out of you.

The door to her office swung open, hitting the doorknob on the back wall with a loud bang. Margo jumped at the sound and whirled on the figure standing in the doorway.

Bill Lint stood uncertainly just outside her office. His face had a pushed-in sort of look, as if someone had drunkenly remolded a wad of dough. His eyes were large and slightly rolling. Margo didn't like to look at him for very long, had even indulged in some shameless ridicule of the man with Jilly at times, although, of course, never within his earshot. He wore baggy, clean blue-jeans and a faded blue-jean shirt buttoned to his throat. Today, he literally fumed with the odor of garlic and onions.

"For God's sakes, what is it?" Tess snapped, rubbing the goose bumps off her arms. "Why don't you knock, for Chrissake?"

"I've done asked you before not to cuss 'round me, Margo." The man spoke in a slow, half-witted drawl, though, as far as Margo knew, he was simply uneducated, not mentally deficient. "I come in here to tell you 'bout the fence in the upper pasture yonder."

"Yes, yes, what is it?" Margo began straightening the unstraightenable pile of receipts and bills on her desk. "What about the fence?" Margo slapped a paperback veterinarian book down on her desk. "Oh, Bill, out with it! I don't have all day."

"Well, excuse me for bothering you." Bill's face clouded with hurt. "I just thought you'd want to know about them horses hurting themselves on that fence with the nails all a-juttin' out like that."

"Nails? What nails?" Margo felt the weight of the planet settle comfortably on her shoulders and she sat down hard in her desk chair. "Which horses?" she asked weakly.

"Well, none's hurt yet," he said self-righteously, "but it's only a matter a time before they find them nails. You know horses. If it's bad for 'em, they'll come onto it sooner or--"

"Yes, yes, Bill. Thanks for letting me know. Now, do you think you could mosey down there and, say, fix the fence before any of our horses find the nails?"

Bill's face brightened again.

"Well, Margo," he said, cheerfully. "You know fixing fences ain't my job. I'm hired to tend the polo fields and nothing else."

Margo wanted to hit the man right over the head with the manure shovel.

"I just thought you'd want to know so's you could get somebody to fix it before some of them expensive horses gets themselves hurt."

"Thank-you, Bill," Margo said quietly, her eyes watching the man as he stood in the door jamb, his meaty hands crossed in front of him like the deformed gnarl of a tree trunk. "I wonder if now you wouldn't mind taking a flying leap--"

"Margo! Great, you're here!" The breathless form of Jessie Parker edged Bill good-naturedly out of the doorway.

Jessie was a bouncing bundle of snarly, gold hair and crinkly blue eyes. She wore her jeans tight, her boots high on her knee, and her jumping helmet--when she bothered to wear it at all--at a positively jaunty angle. Incredibly, the girl groom was as cheerful and affable as she was attractive.

Margo put her head down on her desk.

"Is now not a good time?" Jessie asked, her glittering smile still sparkling away.

"What is it, Jessie?" Margo murmured from the protection of her folded arms.

"I was just wondering if I could exercise Best-Boy? See ya, Bill. Hope I wasn't interrupting anything!" Lint slunk off down the long, dark corridor of the horse barn into the bright sunlight.

"Best-Boy?" Margo said, raising her head slightly.

"Yeah, Jilly's gelding? She never let me ride him before, but, I mean, before he's sold off or whatever, do you think it'd be okay? Margo?"

Margo looked at the fresh-faced girl for a moment and then, surprising both of them, burst into tears.

6

Kazmaroff shifted in the passenger's seat of the car and concentrated on writing in the little spiral-top notebook Burton had tossed onto the dashboard. He shook out his hand and flexed his sore writing fingers.

"God, that woman could talk," he said. "And what kind of rich do you think that is?"

Burton glanced at his partner, unsure of the phrase and therefore annoyed.

"Yeah, that's older-money rich," Kazmaroff said, poising the ball-point over the notebook. "I know her husband brings in a pretty bob or two..."

Burton clenched the steering wheel tighter in his hands.

"...but that palace wasn't bought with attorney's fees."

Burton wanted to scream: *What do you know about it? What do you know what you can buy with attorney's fees? What do you know about old money, for Crissakes?* But he didn't. He stared straight ahead through the windshield and watched the road before him.

"Yep, Miss Portia has done little else with her not-so-young life," Kazmaroff said, underlining key points in his notebook as he spoke, "except ride expensive horses, wear expensive clothes, and listen to landscapers talk about their expensive ideas. God, did you see that contrived forest lining the front drive? She must think she's the Duchess of bloody Windsor."

"Whatever she is or who ever she *thinks* she is," Burton said deliberately, "I know one thing. She's not telling the truth."

Dave straightened in his seat. "What do you mean?" He said. "What part isn't the truth?"

Burton smiled thinly. "I mean," he said, "that she didn't tell us everything."

"Sounded pretty complete to me," Dave said petulantly.

He hates it when I find something before he does, Burton thought pleasantly.

I know how the poor schmuck feels.

"What have we got on the next one?" Burton asked, changing the subject. He knew the Stephens woman was lying, or at least withholding, but he didn't know exactly what. He wasn't about to have his feet held to the fire by Kazmaroff before he was a little closer to the truth himself.

Kazmaroff flipped to the front of his notebook.

"Tess Andersen," he read. "Thirty-eight, never been married, rich." He shrugged. "She's had her horse at the barn for two years now--"

"Rich, how?"

Kazmaroff read his notes.

"A trust. Left to her by her father. Coca-Cola money, I think, from her Grandfather. I don't have the exact figure. Suffice to say, the woman doesn't have to work at the local Piggly-Wiggly in order to afford her barn board."

"Anything else?" Burton sighed and felt the tension creep back into his hands. Why couldn't Kazmaroff just give the facts without all the cutesy-commentary? As if Burton cared what Kazmaroff thought of rich, idle women. As if he cared for his opinion on trust-fund babies.

"Has a Master's degree in French from Yale"

Burton said nothing.

"Wild, huh? Portia Stephens stopped after her junior year at Ol' Miss."

"And Jilly?"

"Business degree from Georgia."

"What? No MBA for Miss Hard Drivin' Business Gal?"

"I don't think she needed it." Kazmaroff tapped the notebook against his knee and watched the scenery out the window. Tall Georgia pines scraped the sky as they drove. "She had something better or as good, you know? Why go back to school when everyone in business is falling all over themselves to be your client? She had a natural way in business."

"Where'd you get that? Prelim interviews with co-workers?"

"Phone work." Kazmaroff shrugged.

"Not bad."

Kazmaroff nearly gave himself whiplash whirling around to look at Burton.

"What else on Tess Andersen?" Burton asked, ignoring his reaction.

Kazmaroff returned to his notebook. "She had some ideas of riding with the U.S. Olympic team at one time."

"You're kidding."

"And now she just sort of rides and has lunch with friends and does some traveling. No husbands, no current boyfriends, no family."

"Interesting."

"Oh, yeah, I found out something else. She's had a face-lift."

"How'd you find that out?"

"People like to talk about that kind of thing." Kazmaroff tossed the notebook in the glove box. "One of the boarders at the barn mentioned it to me. She sounds like a classic stereotype."

Burton pulled up to the guardhouse of the heavily-landscaped entrance of St. Ivan's. North Atlanta's exclusive and largest subdivision, St. Ivan's was a Gotham city of luxury residential homes, most featuring multiple chimneys, palladium windows as large as any cathedral's, and at least three, and usually four, stories of towering brick and stucco.

They were directed to Tess Andersen's address at the back of the subdivision, a stylish brick Traditional with a blood-red Infinity convertible in the curving drive. Once inside, Tess sat on the pale lime damask couch in the living room facing the two detectives. The room itself was a pleasant recreation of springtime in the midst of the Georgia autumn. Pastels and hushed whites swathed the room in a cocoon of coolness and peacefulness. The afternoon sun invaded from the west through an impressive palladium window that covered one wall. Through the window--its warmth and brightness doing little to usurp the design of the room's intensive chill--they could see the tile roofs of Tess' prosperous or well-born neighbors.

Burton had known beautiful women before. Had even sent a few of them to jail where they would age a lot less gracefully than their less pretty sisters. Tess Andersen was certainly beautiful. Her hair was blonde, like Portia's. But, unlike Portia's careful curls, Tess's hair was long and untreated to hours in a beauty salon. It hung to her waist in a sheet of shimmering gold, its highlights flecks of darker topaz and amber which shifted and moved as she did. Her face was oval and delicate, with a small perfect nose, large blue-green eyes, and lips full and sensuous.

She seemed open and friendly and extremely attentive, even offering them cocktails although she must have known through countless television shows that they would refuse. (Did the woman watch television? Burton wondered, looking around the room). He found himself aware of the uncomfortable sensation of becoming convinced that this woman could have had nothing to do with what had happened last Tuesday afternoon. He forced himself to harden.

"Where should I start?" she asked them, her hands cool and calm in her lap. "What can I tell you? You've already spoken with Portia, right?"

Burton nodded. "We'd like to hear it from you," he said.

Tess pushed back a curtain of blonde hair with her hand and Burton noticed she wore no jewelry, not even a watch. Her fingers were manicured, her wrists fragile-looking. He tried to imagine those delicate hands reining in a 1500-pound horse.

"Well," she began, her eyes looking over the detectives' heads to a gilt-framed Auguste Macke on the wall behind them. "We all rode out together about two o'clock, I guess..."

"Did you ride together often?" Kazmaroff wrote as he spoke, not looking at her.

"Umm, yes," Tess said.

Kazmaroff looked up.

"'Ummm,' you're not sure?"

Tess smiled at him and Burton was aware again of how lovely she was. Her eyes blinked into half crescents when she smiled.

"We rode together often, yes," she said, smiling at him.

"Did you get along well with your riding companions, Miss Andersen?" Burton asked.

"Who couldn't get along with Portia? She wants to please more than my old springer, Daisy."

"And Jilly?"

"I imagine you detectives are good enough to have figured out that Jilly lacked some of Mother Theresa's finer qualities."

"Did you get along with Jilly?" Burton pressed.

"I wouldn't have called us fabulous buddies or anything." Tess's smile was firmly in place. "But we didn't have frequent hair pullings or dirt brawls at the barn or anything." She shrugged. "It would scare the horses."

"You contemplated physically fighting with Jilly Travers upon occasion?" Kazmaroff leaned forward in his chair.

"Forget it, Dave." Burton said, leaning back into his chair. "I believe Miss Andersen is being ironic."

"Yes, thank you, Detective Burton. That's just what I'm being. I hope you don't mind."

"Might prolong our visit a little."

"I don't care if you don't."

Kazmaroff looked from Tess to Burton and back to Tess again. "Did you or did you not get along with Jilly Travers?" Jack noticed he was using his *I'm taking control of the situation* voice and puffing his chest out a bit in order to better reach the most sonorous tones for the job.

"Jilly Travers was a bitch," Tess said with a sigh. "You sure you don't want something to drink? I have iced tea."

"Tea would be good," Burton said.

Kazmaroff looked at him in amazement as Tess moved away to get the tea.

"Detective Kazmaroff?" Tess called. "Tea?"

"Uh...uh, sure," he said before turning back to Burton. "What are you doing here?"

"I'm questioning a witness, Dave." Burton looked around the room, determined not to pay too much attention to his partner.

"A possible suspect, *Jack*," Kazmaroff said, crossing his arms and throwing one ankle over his knee. They waited in silence for Tess to return with the drinks.

"Y'all don't look like the sugar type," she said as she entered the room. She handed them each a tall frosty tumbler of tea. The cubes clinked softly against the glasses. "No, Jilly was a bitch and hard to get a long with and incredibly selfish. Gosh," Tess slid back into her seat and pushed long drapes of hair away from her face again. "I'm trying to think of something nice to say about the woman!"

"If she was so unpleasant, why did you ride with her as often as you did?" Kazmaroff asked.

Tess shrugged. "She was just a body." She blushed immediately when she said it, the image of Jilly's dead body rose up among them. "I mean, she made up numbers for a group. It's always more fun to ride in a group."

"Margo Sherman said you enjoy riding alone more than any of her other boarders," Burton said.

"Margo said that?" Tess smiled again. "I suppose I do. But riding in a group's fun too."

"And last Tuesday?" Kazmaroff asked abruptly. He was clearly getting impatient with the new, laconic style of questioning that Burton seemed to have developed. "You rode in a group last Tuesday afternoon. Would you like to tell us about it now?"

"Absolutely."

Burton noticed, imagined? that Tess's hands twitched just a bit as she spoke.

"We rode out, as I've already told you, around two. Sorry I can't be more specific, I don't wear a timepiece." She held up her bare arm. "We took the trail past the formal polo grounds. You know there's the practice field? And then the groomed grounds. Riders aren't allowed to ride across it unless they're involved in an actual match or something."

"This is enforced?" Burton asked pleasantly, sipping his tea.

"Well, there's a groundskeeper..."

"Bill Lint."

"That's right, and he's, like, always hiding behind bushes and trees, trying to catch you out. I can't tell you how many times he's been the cause of a horse spooking and unseating someone. I'm serious. The man's a menace."

"And so Lint keeps an eye on the polo grounds to make sure no riders traverse it." Kazmaroff said, writing again.

Burton caught some of the words the man was writing down: *check out Lint again.*

"Anyway, we rode past--not through--the polo field into a little copse of trees, well, first you have to go down this rather steep creek embankment. Have you not been to the trail yet?"

"Never mind where we've been, Miss Andersen," Kazmaroff said pleasantly. "Just tell us where you rode."

"Well, we forded the creek. And Jilly's gelding--did you see him at the barn?--he's this big 17-hand monster. A sweetie but way too big for her. But God forbid Jilly should be caught riding something more her size. She was only five-foot three, you know." Tess plumped a heavily fringed pillow and tossed it into the corner of the couch.

"Anyway," she continued. "Best-Boy, that's Jilly's horse, balked a few times at going into the water--a lot of horses don't like water--and I remember she was particularly severe with him. Smacking him with her bat and yelling at him." Tess shrugged and smiled. "The woman really was a pig."

"But you all got across," Kazmaroff said.

"Well, of course, it's not the Rio Grande, for heaven's sake. You know what I think? I think Jilly communicated her tenseness about the creek to her horse and that's why he balked. Everything was fine until she started making such a big deal about it.

"Anyway, after that there's just a little trail and you follow it around...it winds here and there...it's really quite lovely, especially this time of year. The afternoon was cool but the sun was out and it was really a nice little hack. Portia and I both commented on it."

"Not Jilly?" Burton prompted.

"Jilly was still stewing over the creek incident. The woman held a grudge. Even against her horse."

"Against you?" Burton asked.

"Goodness!" Tess threw back her head and laughed. "That's wonderful! Just like in the movies. I'm sort of a suspect, aren't I? I mean, I certainly had the opportunity to do her in, now if y'all can only see a motive, right?"

"*Was* there a motive, Miss Andersen?" Burton said. He looked straight into her eyes.

"I guess, in a general sense, there was. Sure." Tess spoke directly to Burton. "For me, and everyone else who ever met

Jilly. And please stop calling me Miss Andersen. If you really want to make me crack, start saying 'yes m'am' to me."

"Let's just here the facts," Burton said. "What happened after you reached the clearing?"

Tess eased back into the sofa. She glanced at Kazmaroff's vexed expression, and then focused again on the painting on the wall behind their heads. "Well, we came to the clearing...about fifteen, maybe twenty minutes, after the trail. I was first, then Jilly, then Portia."

"What did you fight about?" Burton asked, his eyes never leaving her face.

"Tack," she said.

"Come again?"

"Tack, tack." She waved her hand in the air, "Saddles, bridles...she was nursing an earlier snit over a riding crop that she'd lost and thought Portia or I had something to do with it. The woman was demented."

"Had you?"

"Taken her riding crop? Okay, you caught me. You really *are* good, aren't you?" She laughed. "I didn't take the foolish thing, for heaven's sake. In fact, I was offended that she'd think me so unimaginative--"

"But not so spiteful?"

Tess smiled slowly at Burton. "I wasn't above having a good one on the sour old thing. She knew what I was capable of."

"So, she accused you of stealing her..." Burton began.

"Her *crop*. It's like a whip, you know?"

"Her crop. Was she riding with a crop that day?"

"Ummm, yes, she was. A different one."

"It was found wedged between the horse and saddle when the horse returned to the barn," Burton said.

"I'm not surprised. After Jilly beat the poor creature around the head and shoulders over the stupid creek crossing, she tucked the bat away..."

"The bat?"

"It's just a name for it. It's like a crop only shorter, with less give. Kids use them mostly."

"Go on."

"Anyway, she tucked it away on the trail because she wanted Portia and me to think she didn't need it to make Best-Boy mind. You know, beat the horse senseless with it because he embarrasses you or something at a creek crossing, and then get rid of it in case people think you need it to ride with."

"I see," Burton said, not seeing.

"It doesn't matter, detective," Tess said, gaily. "The horsy set is a strange world of odd argot and ridiculous rules. Jilly's not really the exception when it comes to rude horse people. We are, by definition and tradition, snobby, egocentric and patronizing."

"But the big fight was about her crop," Burton asked, steering her back to the point.

Tess nodded. "Normally, I let her bitching and accusations roll off my back. That day, it worked its way right up my nose. I don't know," she looked thoughtfully. "Maybe it was the way she treated Best-Boy. We had words. It got a little ugly, I guess. And we split. Or rather, she told us to sod off, and we did, with pleasure." She shrugged.

"And Portia Stephens chose to leave with you?"

"She did."

"But she had no argument with Jilly."

"No, and she doesn't dislike Jilly. Something very few people can say, I'm sure."

"But Portia left with you."

"Jilly was like a sometimes friendly pitbull, you know? Me, I don't like pit bulls, period. Portia appreciated Jilly for whatever bizarre features she could see in her that were, I don't know, not detestable. But deep down, she knew she was still a pit-bull." She shrugged again. "Of course, she came with me."

"Did you return to the barn immediately?"

"We did."

"Did you go the same way you came?"

"Yes. it's true there's a circular sort of route on that trail after the clearing, which is really the half-way point. I'm sure you've seen the path, there's only one or two, if you count the trail that leads to the main tractor road, that branch off from the clearing." (Burton made a mental note. He'd only found the one leading to the road.) "And it winds back around east to the barn."

"But you didn't take this trail back."

"No. It wasn't nice. It was too narrow and Bill lives in an old bombed-out trailer along the way there."

"Bill?"

"Bill Lint. The polo grounds keeper. Like I said, he's extremely demented and we all do our best to avoid him."

"What time did you arrive back at the barn?" Kazmaroff had his notebook open again.

"I'd say around half past three or so. More tea?"

Burton shook his head. "This stolen crop of Jilly Travers," he said. "Is this a frequent happening at the barn?"

"What, thefts in general or people taking a piece out of Jilly?"

"Either."

"I wouldn't know about the robbery rate at our barn, detective. I'm afraid you'd have to discuss that with Margo Sherman. I, personally, have never had anything stolen. As for Jilly..." She stood up and straightened the pleats in her long Indian skirt. Burton could see tiny reflectors like diamond shaped mirrors flashing in the room's bright sunlight. "...no one liked the woman. I didn't take her crop, not my style. But I certainly was not indignant that someone else had."

"Are you dismissing us?" Burton stood too but Kazmaroff remained seated.

"Can I do that?"

Burton finally laughed. "We'll have to come back, I'm afraid."

"I don't mind."

Kazmaroff finally heaved himself to his feet, nearly knocking over the empty tea glass he'd set on the small antique side table.

She walked them to the door. Kazmaroff headed off immediately to the car, intent on being the driver for the homeward segment of the day. Tess called out to Burton.

"I know you have to find her killer because it's your job."

"But you can think of better things to do with one's time," he said.

She smiled and said nothing.

Burton turned to join Kazmaroff but not before noticing that Tess's delicate, perfect fingers, resting on the large brass doorknob, were trembling.

Chapter Three

1

"Those lips? Definitely collagen." Kazmaroff jabbed a finger at a county map he had perched on the dashboard as he drove. "Is it 141 where this school is? Or right off Medlock Bridge? Can you tell?"

"What kind of crack is that?" Burton sat tensed and uncomfortable in the passenger's seat. Both windows were rolled down and the late afternoon chill was succeeding in enervating, not invigorating, him.

"No kind of crack, Jack," Kazmaroff sighed and gathered up the map in his right hand. "Just an observation. That is our job, isn't it? To observe? To note? I just noted that the woman....didn't you see her scars? In front of each ear, and the guy must've been good. They were hairline, you could barely..."

"What is the point of this?" Burton turned to face him. "Going to do a gossip column for the Fulton County P.D, are you? Going to write a "Guess Who Saw Who Doing Guess What" for suspects? Get your mind out of *Entertainment Tonight*, why don't you? and back to work. Our job, detective, is not to ascertain who did or did not have a nip or tuck for whatever reasons. Our *job* is to determine the facts in order to determine the identity of the killer and then to arrest said killer. In case you've forgotten."

"Screw you, man," Kazmaroff snarled, his eyes boring a hole through the windshield. "Or, should I say Tess Andersen?"

Burton lunged at him, only able to control himself after the car nearly swerved into a passing Jeep Cherokee. The jeep emitted a long, unhappy beep and then accelerated well past the speed limit to escape them.

"What is your problem, man?" Kazmaroff was scarlet. "You trying to kill us and innocent motorists too?"

"Stop this car, you suck-faced little runt." Burton was apoplectic in his anger and impotence. "Stop this car so I can beat the shit outta you!"

"Oh, man, you are a piece of work." Kazmaroff obviously had no intention of stopping the car for Burton. "You're trying to kill us both...I can't believe the stunt you just pulled--"

"Just shut-up!" Burton said. He gripped his knees with his hands. He imagined Kazmaroff's face in his hands and he was beating it and pounding it, crushing it. "I don't want to hear your voice, your constant noise. Just shut-up."

"Screw you, man," Kazmaroff said, but there was no heat in his words, as if he only felt honor-bound to say them.

Burton pulled himself up straight in his seat and took a deep, covert breath. "I am so sick of your bull-shit," he said tightly, not looking at Kazmaroff. "I'm sick to death of your affectations, your strange foreign accents--who are you supposed to be? friggin' Meryl Streep?--you're pathetic, *Dave*." He licked his lips as he spoke and continued to stare straight ahead out the windshield. "Your pathetic attempts to be something you're not and will never be... You don't play polo, hell, man you don't even ride a bicycle. What you know about wines--this one really kills me--what you know about wines, you could fit in your left *ear*. And you know something else, man? I'm sick of your references to the Gulf War when the closest you've ever been to Iraq is the Middle eastern bakery on Buford Damn Highway."

"Are you through?"

"Fuck you."

"Because if you are, then maybe you'd like to hear how fond I am of *you*. First of all, your moods. Of which you have many."

"I'm warning you, Kazmaroff."

"You are the sourest son of a bitch I ever met. I mean, do you have smile muscles? Is everything just a complete and tremendous pain in the ass for you?"

Burton picked up the map and willed himself to remain calm.

"I've tried," Kazmaroff continued, shaking his head. "I've ignored stuff. I've taken rebuffs, out and out insults. You don't like me, fine. You don't have to like me. Plenty of guys in the department work together and don't like each other. We don't have to do Saturday afternoon barbecues together." Kazmaroff turned the car down a newly-paved road that cleaved the gray shrubs and bushes like a knife. "But now it looks like we can't even do a routine investigation together," he said.

Justin Traver's boarding school stood alone in a tidy woodland setting. A complicated drystone wall, composed of fieldstone, pieces of quarry rock, and red mud, curved around the front of the two-story brick façade of the school. Simple, shuttered windows hung in three rows of eight across the front.

Woodstone Academy was situated on fifty acres. Its curriculum offered students horseback riding, rugby and sailing in addition to the usual football and track programs. The school was expensive, but not prohibitively so. It was less than six miles from the lonely woodland clearing where Jilly Travers disappeared.

Burton and Kazmaroff drove the last five miles in silence, neither of the two willing to break the code they seemed to be forging. A code of separateness. Their appointment was with the headmaster of the school, George Patterson. Tall and affable, Panfel greeted them warmly in his office. Three walls of the office were covered in floor-to-ceiling bookcases, the fourth wall was completely windowed to afford a stunning view of rolling green pastures rimmed by tall pines. Kazmaroff and Burton sat across from the man's desk in a small seating arrangement by the window. Kazmaroff sat in the small leather loveseat which was pocked with serious brass studs as if to definitely declare its maleness. Burton settled down in one of the matching wing back chairs, reserving its twin for Justin Travers. Patterson remained standing, as if to assure the detectives that he would not be in their way for very long.

Kazmaroff smiled politely at the headmaster and slowly opened his notebook. “Has Justin been told about our visit ahead of time, or will this be a surprise?" he asked.

"He has been told," Panfel said, nodding vigorously. "One of our brightest boys. Our very brightest. You'll get articulation-plus with young Travers. Absolutely."

"Well, great," Burton said wryly.

"Fine. I'll just get him, shall I?"

Kazmaroff smiled at the man inoffensively and then, when the headmaster had left, scowled as he glanced about the room.

The silence was palpable.

Moments later, the door opened and they were joined by Jilly Traver's only relative, her son, Justin.

Neither detective stood when the boy entered. Kazmaroff motioned him to take the last remaining seat between them.

The boy was good-looking. Fifteen years old, dark-haired with even darker eyes. The pupils of his eyes were invisible in dark pools of mahogany brown.

Kazmaroff frowned in what Burton took to be his best stab at an affect of compassion with a touch of professional detachment. Burton thought he looked confused.

"Justin Travers?" Burton said, smiling economically.

"Obviously," Justin said staring directly, confidently at Burton.

Burton gave him a sharp look. "Sorry about your mother," he said. "You know that's why we're here today."

The boy said nothing. His eyes flitted away from the detectives and around the room. He seemed on-guard, watchful, to Burton. He did not seem very broken up by the possibility of his mother's death.

"We need to ask you a few questions, Justin," Burton continued, annoyed with the boy's cool behavior.

"I'll make it easy for you," Justin said, his gaze returning to Burton. "I'm not at all sorry she's dead. Okay? There was no love lost. We weren't close. Not in a good way, anyhow."

"You were close in a bad way?" Kazmaroff asked, still frowning.

"You'd be surprised," the boy replied. "I suppose that statement considerably changes the tenor of your questions, huh? I mean, you can skip over the bereavement part of your presentation and get right into the meat of 'did I know of anyone who might want to harm my mother?' Yeah, I mean, I thought of doing it myself, for one."

"You wished your mother dead?" Burton asked as he leaned back into his chair.

Justin's gaze never wavered from Burton's face. "I hated the bitch," he said flatly.

2

"Can you believe that shit?" Kazmaroff shifted into third gear. It caught for a moment before falling into place and Burton winced at the resultant grinding noise. "Doesn't know who his father is? Says his mother used to set her friends up to seduce him? Says his mother used to try to seduce him herself? Is this kid for real?"

Burton wished he had a cigarette. He wondered how long before the urge really went away. He'd already been off them for nearly a year and he still craved them on a more or less daily basis.

"My guess, the kid is a psychopathic liar, you know?" Kazmaroff continued.

Burton sighed and looked out the window at the North Fulton County countryside rolling by. The brown and gray pastures were now punctuated with the occasional grocery store, large and vault-like, with a scattering of cars in the cement parking lots. Jack wondered how they managed to stay in business.

"Based on what?" Burton asked methodically.

"Based on the pure hooey he was spinning." Kazmaroff turned his head toward Burton. "You buying all that stuff about being seduced by these middle-aged women? It's a teenage boy's fantasy. Can you imagine your friend Miss Andersen coming on to that pimply-faced little punk?"

Burton suppressed a wince. He knew it had been coming. Justin had insisted that he'd slept with Tess--at Tess's insistence, he said--when he was only thirteen. It was too much to hope that Kazmaroff wouldn't fixate on it.

"I don't know what to think," Burton said. "We're just gathering facts at this point."

"Bull-shit," Kazmaroff said. "We're gathering the facts and testing people's reactions and using our guts to see who's lying. Don't tell me you haven't got a read on that kid. You think he's telling the truth?"

Burton shook his head. "I don't know," he repeated.

Kazmaroff made a sound of disgust and they drove in silence.

Burton stared out again at the bleak landscape. It was amazing to him the number and variety of birds he'd noticed just forty miles north of town. He'd forgotten so much. Used to be a time he could name them all, sketch them perfectly. When he was a boy, on a warm fall day, much like this one, he and his father could sit for hours watching and waiting. He had delighted his scholarly father with his interest in birds, his patience. The two had been so much alike in all the ways that were important. And then, years later, with everything that had happened in between, he'd decided to make the police force his career. The look in his father's eyes when he told him was like a betrayal.

It was ludicrous, of course, that the boy and Tess Andersen....but why was the kid trying to implicate himself? He had no alibi for the time of Jilly's disappearance, his school was less than six miles from the barn, and he made it clear he did not grieve her. Why? Was he trying to protect someone else?

The name "Tess" came maddeningly to mind and Burton thrust it away. Maybe the kid was just troubled. He certainly hadn't been able to shed any light on the case or Jilly's whereabouts. Justin said he hadn't seen his mother in well over a month.

Burton set his mouth in a grim line and gripped the straps of his seat belt. It was the ex-husband they needed to be talking to, he thought. And soon. This kid was a total waste of time. In more ways than one.

That's my read on it, Dave ol' bud.

The husband was always the first suspect in any investigating cop's mind--no matter of how unlikely, initially, that looked. In this case, there being no husband to point the finger at, the ex-husband, Mark Travers, would have to do.

Feeling a little better, Burton glanced at his partner who looked like he was in the full form of an adult sulk. Deciding he felt even better, Burton was about to suggest they stop somewhere for lunch when his cell phone rang.

"Burton, here," he said.

Kazmaroff tapped his fingers impatiently against the steering wheel. "Well?" he said.

Burton gave him an 'in a minute' wave with his free hand and spoke into the phone. "Okay, good, yeah, no kidding. Okay, thanks." He hung up.

"That was the crime lab," he said. "The blood's definitely her blood-type. No way to make a definite match?"

"Not without a body, tissue, something."

“I don’t suppose Jilly would have made things easy on us by having a supply of her blood stored at one of the local hospitals for some reason?”

“I guess we could check. The Chief said we’re to treat it officially as a homicide. No way she could've lost all that blood and still be breathing somewhere."

A red-tailed hawk circled deliberately in the sky as they drove back to the city. Burton felt his spirits lift at the sight, surprised at his own reaction. Spotting hawks this far out of town was certainly not uncommon, he admonished himself. He watched the bird swoop down on his prey like a dive bomber.

But, oh, so satisfying.

3

Jilly tossed her long hair and smiled her most honest-looking smile. Her eyes blazed directly into his own. Her eyes said "eat me up." Her tongue, flicking the lips of her smile said: "Hurry."

Robert Shue rubbed his forehead with a callused hand and pushed the image of Jilly from his mind. Whatever she'd been, whatever she may or may not have been saying at that motel in Santa Monica three months ago, was a moot point now. He stood up and walked from his desk to the floor-to-ceiling window in his office that overlooked Peachtree Road. It was after eight o'clock and the street was streaked with red and yellow streamers from car tail lights as people prepared for their weekend. With the exception of himself, the offices of Ryan, Davis & Shue were empty.

Jilly.

He allowed himself to remember her the last time he ever laid eyes on her. She had frowned in surprise to see him, hardly expecting him there of all places, on her turf. Her body and face said immediately and irrevocably what her lips had been telling him for weeks.

It's over.

He let himself feel the anger, the humiliation, wash over him once more, just as it had then. But only now did he recall that the contempt in her face had relaxed into a softer, less repulsed, expression. She had smiled the old smile at him. Just for a minute, she had summoned a different kind of feeling than the impatience and irritation the dying relationship had fostered. He'd felt it now, had seen it then but hadn't recognized it. By then, of course, if had been too late. Way, way too late.

Shue fingered the square phone message slip in his pocket. His secretary had scribbled on it as mindlessly as if it had been just another reminder note from a creditor, a "job well done" from a client, or a "call-home" from his wife, Sandra, instead of the end of his world as surely as a bullet in the brain. The police had called. They had called and asked that he please return their call.

"I love you, Jilly. Don't you know I do?"

"So, is this, like, a proposal or something?"

She'd worn nothing. As comfortable and confident in her nakedness as most people would have been in an Armani suit. She was lounging on the motel bed, lighting a cigarette. For a moment, Shue could imagine a tiny cinder from the end of her cigarette falling lightly on that smooth, hard abdomen. He had no doubt she wouldn't have flinched, possibly not even have felt it.

He'd laughed nervously.

"Jilly, I'm married. You know that."

"So this I-love-you stuff is, what? Guilt? An addendum to dinner?"

"Christ."

"Because it certainly isn't necessary, Barry." She laughed and blew the smoke out of her nose in two thin streams. "Now, the dinner," she said. "That was necessary!"

He'd made a mistake. A big mistake. Not in sleeping with her, although that had prompted its own complications in the long run. Not even in his becoming as attached to her as he had. She was right, of course. It wasn't love. It was something else. Something that assuaged a need in him that had been growing for a long time. Something beyond the abilities of his marriage, the love of his wife, or the love for his wife.

No, the mistake had to do with secrets. Secrets told, secrets betrayed. He'd trusted her. That was his big mistake.

4

The little cedar-fronted ranch house was situated back from the street. Hickory and pine trees towered over it, casting shadows even on the sunniest days. Burton had made some effort to keep the bayberry hedges that lined the little drive to the carport neat or, at least, alive; they squatted in single file, in varying sizes and conditions of health.

He stood on the small porch and took a long drag from a cigarette. It was old and stale and felt like it was clawing its way down his throat, but he still found himself pinching the filter to force more nicotine up into the draw.

Inside, he could hear the laugh-track of the sit-com from the television set in the living room. He didn't hear his wife laugh or react in any way to the show. He knew she was sitting in front of the set, a Danielle Steele in her lap, a glass of Coca-

Cola, no ice, on the arm of the couch. In his mind, he saw her concentrating on the commercials in between the shows with as much intensity as the shows themselves. He took a hard drag on the Salem. Maybe that wasn't fair, he thought. Probably wasn't.

He looked out onto the quiet street. It was working class, nothing fancy. Tidy. The people here cared about their lawns, their shrubs, keeping their dogs and kids carefully fenced in. There were one or two houses a couple streets over with the required car up on cement blocks, a major construction job being plotted out in someone's side yard, a child's swing set--the use of which had stripped a once-green lawn of every blade of grass. But here, on Claremont Terrace, things were tidy.

He thought of David Kazmaroff's face as he'd seen it this afternoon, twisting in disgust and affected weariness.

"Is this, like, big breaking news or something?" Kazmaroff had said in response to the call from the lab. "We're supposed to treat this as a murder?"

It didn't matter. Burton pinched off the lit end of the cigarette and ground it out on the porch. He flipped the butt into the Rose of Sharon bush that bordered the tiny porch. Dana had planted azaleas one year, even annuals--pansies or something--that lined the broken sidewalk that led to the front door. Must have been the year they moved in, over seven years ago now. There hadn't been much planting of any kind since then. It was enough, Burton thought as he listened to the screech of the laugh track, just to keep what they had alive.

Kids might've helped. They seemed like a big pain in the ass, but who knows? They might've helped.

His neighbor from across the street pulled into his driveway and waved. Burton returned the wave, trying to remember the guy's first name. Bill or Dale. He'd long since stopped remembering people's first names. The guy was German or something. Spoke with an accent. A Carolina Wren sang out from somewhere in the porch eaves. He'd always loved their song. So distinctive, so cheerful. The rush of Burton's next thought was forceful enough that he actually gasped, shocking himself by the sound in the still evening air. An image of Tess Andersen had come to mind. Her eyes, bold and suggestive, her nude body twisting on the ground in a sensuous stretch. The fragrance of fresh hay and feed seemed to hang gently but undeniably in the air where Jack stood on his porch.

Jesus.

He licked his lips and patted his shirt pocket for cigarettes he knew were not there. Was that bastard Kazmaroff right? Was he losing his objectivity about this woman? Why was she getting to him? There was a connection between them that he couldn't explain. A connection that had been there immediately, would have been there if they'd met each other for the first time at the local Kroger. It was powerful and immediate and he found himself trusting it. His eyes sought out the dark form of his German neighbor as the man knelt in his driveway to examine a tire of his Volvo.

And, unfortunately, what he was feeling had absolutely nothing to do with the fact that Tess Andersen was under suspicion for murder.

5

The night was unusually warm for this time of year. The pasture horses, as if sensing the lagniappe, were particularly playful. The pecking order of the small herd of twenty pasture-boarded horses had been painfully and completely established with the immediate introduction of each new horse to the group.

Now they grazed and interacted with fluidity and certainty, each member knowing its place. The leader, a surly black horse that was gelded late, enjoyed the warm October evening by stampeding his herd up and down the hilly east side of the pasture, stopping abruptly each time they reached the woods which bordered the fenced end of the field. Occasionally, the black gelding would lean over and nip one of the other horses, often a mare, although mating was not an issue.

Stallions were never boarded at Bon Chance. Too much trouble, Margo thought as she watched the horses thunder past her office window. Altogether too much trouble.

The last of the Jeep Cherokees and Mercedes sports vehicles had loaded up their exhausted, dirty children with their hobbit-sized saddles an hour ago and departed in a noisy wagon train of kids, mothers and pedigreed dogs. Sometimes, Margo didn't know how she could stand another day of it.

She turned her eyes away from the horses in the pasture and stood up. She felt every inch of her forty-five years tonight. It had been a hard day. A hard week. She opened her office door and went out into the darkened corridor of the stalls. The light from her office cut a single shaft of brightness into the hallway, illuminating the straw and dirt that made up the floor. A horse in the stall to her left nickered gently and poked his nose out over his stall door. Margo absently touched his velvety nose and murmured to him. Then, she went down the hall to the tenth stall and opened the door. In the corner stood a giant chestnut horse. He had a sweet face and kind eyes. He turned his head, to watch her approach.

"Hello, boy," she said, gently, putting a slow hand up to touch his neck. "How you doing tonight, guy? Had a good dinner, I see."

Margo picked up one of the dandy brushes from the window sill, silently filing away an admonishment for Jessie for leaving it there, and began to groom the animal. Jilly had had him bought him in Ireland two years ago and had him shipped over. He was trained as a hunter but Jilly never hunted him. A Clydesdale-Thoroughbred mix, he stood over 22 hands tall--his back easily level with Margo's head--yet he moved with the grace and lightness of a Springbok. Margo knew what Jilly had paid for him and she personally believed he was worth every penny and probably more. He was not only an elegant mover, perfectly trained and always in balance, but he was sweet-tempered. A rare combination in a horse.

She brushed his saddle area, although she could tell Jessie had already cleaned him thoroughly, then moved down to his flanks and finally, his legs, with more gentle strokes. He was, in fact, a horse of a lifetime. Eager when you needed enthusiasm, quiet when you needed a break. A damn near perfect horse. A horse to die for.

Not for the first time, Margo was struck by the contrast between rider and mount. Of course, Jilly would demand the best, and Best Boy certainly was that. He didn't begrudge his rider as so many horses do--even beautifully trained, expensive horses--but genuinely seemed to enjoy being ridden. Remarkable. And he had been owned by one of the nastiest, unhappiest riders to ever lift a leg into a saddle. As she ran her fingers through his silky mane Margo surprised herself by the sudden knowledge that she would give anything to own him. She wondered what was to be done with him now.

Finally, she gave him a plug of carrot which he took, crunching noisily. She patted him on the neck.

"Sleep well, beauty," she said softly. "We'll get you some exercise tomorrow."

After carefully securing his stall door and checking briefly on another horse that a boarder had had the vet up to see that afternoon, Margo went back to her office. She checked her watch. It was almost nine o'clock. As she approached her office, she could hear the phone ringing and she broke into a trot. She caught the phone receiver up, tripping over a tangle of leather training reins and a lunge line she'd dropped on the floor earlier.

"Yes?" she said breathlessly into the phone.

"Hey, Margo, it's me." The voice was tired, anemic, familiar.

Margo turned and kicked the office door shut. She slumped onto the couch facing the desk and held the phone with both hands.

"Jesus," she said, closing her eyes. "I prayed this would be you. Are you okay?"

"I killed her, Margo," the voice said.

Chapter Four

1

"Mark? What are you talking about?" Margo felt her hands grow cold.

"I'm telling you...oh, Margo, what am I going to do?" The voice on the line became suddenly strident.

"I can't believe I killed the bitch...after so many years of dreaming about it and now I can't believe she's really dead and that I'm going to go to prison for doing her!
I think I'm going mad, Jesus, Margo, do you think I could plead insanity? I mean, do you think if I explained all the shit she's put me through, the judge would understand?"

"You really killed her?" Margo gasped.

"Yes...yes, I...what the hell have we been talking about here? Yes, I killed her. Jesus, Margo, are you just now getting the picture? I killed her! I killed the bitch!"

"Settle down, Mark," she said. She caught herself searching the wall to find the picture of him; happy, young, married to Jilly. "Let me just take all this in. Have you talked to the police?"

"No! They want to, but I've been avoiding them."

"They won't let you do that forever."

"I know, I know. You've talked to them, what do they sound like? Do they sound like they have a suspect? Do they talk like they know who did it?"

"I can't believe you killed her, Mark. I'm stunned." A soft noise shifted somewhere in her swirl of thoughts and senses. Somewhere in the stable. "I mean, how? And why?"

"You, of all people, can ask me why?"

Margo tried to imagine him rubbing his face with his hand, gnawing at a bitten-down fingernail. She could imagine his handsome face puckered with annoyance, even guilt. She couldn't picture the expression on his face that would accompany this conversation.

"I thought it was just talk," she said, tiredly. "It never occurred to me that you...I mean...that you could cold-bloodedly..."

"I didn't actually do it with my bare hands, Margo. Christ, you think I'm an animal or something?"

Margo didn't reply. She heard a muffled scraping noise coming from the other side of her office. It stopped almost as soon as she tried to listen for it.

"...she was going to ruin me this time. I can't even tell you what she wanted to do. But you know Jilly, right, Margo? You know what she was into. Humiliation, torture..."

"Mark, you need to talk to the police." Margo felt her head begin to swim. She tried to remember if she'd eaten lunch.

"Fuck the police! I killed her, Margo! I can't talk to the *police*! Can you see me talking to the police? They're going to nail me, man! My ass is dead-meat if I talk to the police! I got to find a place to--"

The scream came from somewhere in the barn; erupting in a crescendo of pure terror. Margo dropped the phone and jerked open the door that divided her office from the rest of the barn. She could hear Mark continue to talk as if unaware that the phone had bounced down off the desk on her end and was now laying on the floor amid an opened box of worming paste samples. The screams continued. They were coming from the last stall just before the outer gate. Margo ran down the darkened aisle, her sneakers thudding softly in the straw and dust.

It was Traveler's stall. He was a gentle, elderly quarter-horse mix breed that belonged to a woman who rarely rode him. When Margo reached his stall, the horse was backing up against the rear slats of his stall, his eyes white and rolling with fear, as he screamed.

"Whoa, Tray, boy...whoa, there, Traveler. What's the matter, boy?"

Margo opened the stall gate and held her hand out to the animal, trying to calm it. The horse seemed to recognize her. Worried that he might hurt himself in the close confines of his stall, Margo slowly reached inside the stall for the lead rope that was hanging on its hook.

She quickly snapped it to the horse's halter. Without entering the small stall, Margo gave the lead a firm tug and the horse sprang into the center aisle of the barn, nearly on top of her.

Margo jumped back, away from the frantic animal, still holding onto the lead rope.

"Hey, boy, it's okay, it's okay," she murmured to him, wondering where the hell Jessie was, or if Lint were nearby to hear the noise.

The large bay horse suddenly whirled to face Margo, then, without warning, reared up on its back legs, blotting out the hanging overhead lamp in the barn. Margo only saw the horse as a terrible, dark shadow as he flailed his hooves wildly in the air, finally coming down hard and missing her feet by inches.

Trapped against the back of the barn passageway, Margo flung down the lead rope in a sudden panic and tried to decide if she had a chance of slipping past the animal to the lighted paddock at the end of the barn. From there, even if Traveler wheeled after her, she could dive under the fence and be safe.

Margo shouted for help and eyed the distance to the paddock. Suddenly, the crazed animal reared again. Margo crossed her face with her forearms. His front hooves came down hard, striking her solidly in the face and chest, knocking her arms aside and crushing her to the ground.

2

The polo field stretched to the horizon like a piece of emerald-green velvet. Portia was in her car, on the way to the stable for an early evening ride. Unusual for her, to ride alone and so late in the day. She caught a glimpse of her reflection in the car's rear view mirror and saw that she'd forgotten to take off her earrings. They were long, gold chains with swinging clusters of pearls at the end.

She made a face. She must look ridiculous dressed in breeches and paddock boots with dangling earrings on!

She stopped the car next to the polo field and unscrewed them, tossing them impatiently in her ash tray. Can't even hack the perimeter of the polo grounds, she thought with annoyance, with all the police still everywhere. At the thought of the police, her mind flashed a picture of Tess. How she wished she didn't have to remember things, think of things. She resumed driving her car down the long driveway and parked in front of the middle barn. She saw Margo's Saturn but no other cars. The light was fading quickly. It would be totally dark before she'd even tacked up. She'd have to ride in the ring with the overhead lights on. She sighed heavily.

Why couldn't Tess just tell the police that she'd gone back to Jilly that afternoon but hadn't found her? Why did she have to insist that Portia lie for her? It was too nerve-wracking. She had a good mind to just tell the police the truth.

That she and Tess had split up less than a half a mile after they'd left Jilly. That Tess had said she was going back to make it up with Jilly--as if anybody would believe that!--hadn't found her, and had come on back to the stables alone. It was simple and left Portia completely out of it. It was all so selfish on Tess's part.

Portia opened her Mercedes trunk and pulled her Crosby Prix Des Nations close contact saddle onto the lip. She felt in the bottom of the trunk for her girth and bridle. The sun had completely set now. Somewhere in the stable, she heard a noise. She paused to listen, and the sound wasn't there.

She looked over in the direction of Margo's apartment. The lights were out but her car was there. Just to the east of Margo's place, Portia could see the strips of yellow police tape barring the entrance to one of the pastures.

The autumn will be gone, she thought dully, as she turned back to her car to finish unloading, before they let us ride the polo fields again.

3

"She'll live." Kazmaroff spoke briefly into his phone from where he stood in the hallway off the nurse's station, the busy hospital corridor behind him.

The nursing shifts were in the process of changing. The nurses sat in a group behind the long desk of the nurse's station. The graveyard shift was tiredly briefing the early morning crew over styrofoam cups of steaming coffee as to the status of each of the patients during the night.

Burton nodded in response on the other line. He was at police headquarters, had been since a little before five that morning. He watched the suspect inside the interrogation room through a sound-proof window where the man sat carefully chewing every fingernail on both hands.

"Who found her?"

"Portia Stephens. She called the fucking *vet*."

"Oh, well."

"What was Portia doing at the barn?"

"Intending to ride, it seems."

"At eight o'clock at night? Okay," he said. He rubbed his eyes. It had already been a long day.

"But the little barn girl...what's her name?"

"Jessie."

"Yeah, she's here at the hospital. She showed up at the barn at about the same time the paramedics did. Says she was supposed to go over some stuff with Margo. She says that horse is as gentle as a butterfly. She says there's no way that horse would've stomped her."

"Is there some question as to which horse did the stomping?"

"No, it was that horse all right."

"Then what is she suggesting? That the horse was drugged?"

"The vet's running tests on him and his feed now. What about the ex-husband?" Kazmaroff asked, switching the subject. "Getting anything?"

Burton laughed. He looked back at the man visible through a one-way mirror sitting inside the interrogation room.

"You might say that," he said.

Surprised at Burton's light tone, Kazmaroff hesitated, then: "Okay, try me."

"He confessed to wanting to kill her..."

"Yeah?"

"He confessed, even to contracting to *have* her killed."

"You're kidding."

"But, in the end, he insists, quite tearfully, I might add, that he did *not* kill her."

"I'll bet he does."

"It's even better." Burton found himself remarkably un-irritated with Kazmaroff this morning and wondered if perhaps they needed to deal with each other primarily via telephone in future. "He says he called the hit-man to see if he had done the deed only to find out the guy was waiting for the check to clear before he did anything."

Kazmaroff burst out laughing. Burton laughed too and was aware that it was the first time in four years of working together that the two of them had ever shared a laugh. It made him feel slightly nauseated.

"The dumb bastard accepted a check?" Kazmaroff asked, still laughing.

"Yeah, the hit-man's as stupid as the ex-husband."

"What are you going to do?'

"Let him cool his well-heeled heels awhile," he said. "I can hold him a few more hours so I thought I'd run down another lead and let him sit here and chew his fucking nails down to the knuckles."

"What lead?"

The tension snapped back between them as quickly and palpably as a rubber band shot from a sling.

"Just something. Probably nothing."

"Why don't you bore me with it? Since we are both working this case together?"

"I told you--"

"Give me a break, man!" Kazmaroff snarled. "You've been telling me all along the husband's the one. Now he turns up with a fucking confession and you're tracking down some other lead? I don't believe it. Listen, you want to take personal time off, just say so, don't give me any bull-shit about following some lead you--"

Burton held his temper and carefully, purposefully, broke the connection.

4

Tess returned the phone to its cradle. Her brow was pinched in an expression of worry and fear. She walked to the hall mirror in her condo and stood there a moment, reflecting on the phone conversation, and on the face she saw before her.

Quietly, she reached into the drawer of the hall table that sat under the mirror and pulled out a tube of lipstick. She applied the bright color to her lips, smudging the corner of her mouth with her shaking hand.

She stared into the mirror, watching the fine lines criss-crossing her eyes. A tiny vein pulsed unattractively under one eye and the lipstick looked garish against her too-pale face. She continued to stare into the mirror.

Fuck you, Jilly, she thought.

5

Burton tossed the notebook on the desk and eased back into his desk chair. His mind fought to push the personal agendas out and back and away. He turned to stare at a photograph of the crime site. Without even a corpse to help keep him focused, he forced himself to concentrate on examining the bloody setting of Jilly's last moments on earth.

He and Kaz had combed the area surrounding the farm in a perimeter measuring nearly a half mile.

Burton knew, of course, that there was no reason to believe she hadn't been buried a little further out, or stuffed in a car trunk and dumped in the Chattahoochee, for that matter. But the bloodhounds had covered an even wider area with no joy. As a result, they'd eliminated the actual stables as a possibility for Jilly's last resting place. After all, she would have to have been killed, then dragged back to the barn area and buried or hidden, in the middle of people saddling horses and taking lessons and driving in and out. He shook his head. It didn't make sense.

Before the attack on Margo, he had searched the clearing, two barns, all the stalls and even had the pond dragged. They'd brought bloodhounds in to cover the entire area. Nothing. No body. No murder weapon. Burton had checked all three pastures to see if anything had been freshly buried in one of them.

The attack on Margo had forced him to cordon off the barn buildings again. This time, it wasn't just a look-see; they'd be taking careful samples of everything from the blood on the straw floor to the mouse droppings that went with it.

Stupid!

Burton tossed the photograph down in disgust. He wasn't paying attention these days, he was logging in his time, there in body and not much more. He wondered how badly he'd compromised the case so far, and made a note to be on hand later in the afternoon when forensics combed the tack rooms and stalls.

He stood up and stretched his back. It wasn't yet ten in the morning. He planned on keeping Mark Travers in the interrogation room another four hours at least. The man had wept nearly the whole interview earlier that morning with Burton. And it wasn't because he mourned his ex-wife.

Funny, Burton mused, the thing that he and Kazmaroff had found so amusing--the only thing, in fact, they had ever found amusing in tandem--was the one thing, i.e.--making fun of Mark Travers--that was loaded to the gunnels with coincidental ironies. For example, although Burton had no doubt that Kaz was genuinely disgusted with the stupidity (not to mention depravity) of Travers' actions, the two detectives had laughed, in large part, because they were enjoying ridiculing a member of a moneyed social class--the very class that Kazmaroff attempted on a daily basis to pass himself off as a card-carrying member of.

Burton scratched his head and lifted a cold cup of coffee to his lips. He'd never thought about it before but maybe there was something more complicated behind Dave wanting to grace the cover of "Town & Country." And if *that's* true, and it's really a lack of self-confidence covered up by the avalanche of reeking swagger that he, Burton, was continually repulsed by, then maybe, just maybe, there was a glimmer of a possibility that they might have a meeting point. After all.

Like I give a shit, Burton thought with a grimace, and tossed the coffee in his trash can.

The phone rang on his desk. It was Kazmaroff.

"I'm leaving here, Jack," Kazmaroff said, obviously choosing to ignore the way their last conversation had terminated.

"Great, go out to the barn. I'll be out in a couple of hours."

"After you check out your private lead."

"That's been moved to this evening."

"You don't want to admit she's involved and man, you know she is up to her surgically-tightened neck! She's not a witness, Jack! She's a fucking suspect! Are you crazy or something?"

Burton forced himself to look back at the photograph on his desk, the mangled tall grass doused with crimson. He tried to bring a picture to mind of Jilly doing something... what? in that clearing. Instead, he saw himself and Tess lying nude in the grass. He was kissing her, stroking her bone-white skin.

Stop it! Stop it!

"You still there, Jack?"

"Yeah." It was a croak more than a voice.

"You always liked the ex-husband as the perp, right? Well, you got him; you've talked to him, and you can't see it, can you?"

"No," Jack admitted. "First impressions only."

"Sometimes that's all a detective's got."

"Funny how poorly that tends to hold up with the D.A."

"You know what I'm talking about. If you're going to interview Tess Andersen without me, you gotta be thinking she could've done it, damn it! Is that what you're thinking, Jack? Is it?"

"I'll be at the barn after twelve," Burton replied. "Coordinate with the agent until I get there. Make sure every blade of straw, every lump of horse shit ends up in a box or a baggie, check out every splinter or injury any one got after the attack on Margo. And talk to Lint and Jessie again."

"Yeah, right. See you at twelve." Kazmaroff's voice was full of disgust.

Burton hung up, then walked to the window of his office. He had a beautiful view of the parking lot. He turned and picked up the phone and gave orders to have Mark Travers released after three o'clock. Then he called home to tell his wife he'd have to work late tonight.

6

The martini was ice-cold, with three olives. It was Tess's second. Burton hadn't appeared yet and she felt she needed the fortification.

Mia Spago's was nearly empty, as she expected it would be on an early Thursday evening. Tess sat at the bar, her profile to the restaurant's main entrance.

She wore a pale gray Armani jacket over a silk blouse and jeans. She'd taken some time deciding what to wear tonight. She didn't want to appear to be the rich-bitch party girl she was sure Dave Kazmaroff was advising his partner she was. A Gucci pin held a Milanese shawl in place across her right shoulder and breast. She lit another cigarette.

"Another martini?"

She shook her head at the bartender who moved away, polishing glasses.

She hated feeling this way. Why couldn't she just think of him as a man instead of a cop? *Relax, darling*, she told herself. *He won't come as a cop tonight. You know he won't.*

"Been waiting long?"

Burton was at her elbow and Tess fought an impulse to check to see if he were wearing sneakers.

"Oh! You surprised me. I expected you to come through the front door."

Burton motioned to the bartender.

"Whatever the lady's having."

He seated himself at the bar next to her.

"You okay?" he asked her, frowning. "You look a little shaky."

Tess forced herself to keep her hands quiet.

"Well," she said trying to sound light and joky, "it is a little like withdrawal, not being able to ride."

"It's just temporary. He's being well-taken care of."

"I can't imagine he is. By that stupid Margo? I've forbidden her to even dream of getting on Wizard. The last thing I need is for her to undo months of training by one little hack-among-friends along the back trails."

"I didn't know you didn't like Margo."

"I..." Tess took a sip of her drink as the bartender brought Burton his.

"I've always wanted to try one of these," Burton said.

Tess blinked as if he'd suddenly lapsed into Urdu.

"A martini?" she said.

"Yeah, I'm kind a domestic-brew guy, I guess."

"Oh, well, anyway, I mean...it's not that I don't like Margo. I guess she does her job well enough, but she constantly wants to be friends, you know?"

"Is that a pretty repulsive idea, I guess?"

Tess blushed and smiled at Burton.

"Am I being questioned formally tonight?" she asked sweetly.

"Sorry."

Burton set down his martini and picked up Tess' hand, surprising her, calming her, which surprised her again.

"Margo was attacked last night at the barn."

Tess withdrew her hand and put it to her mouth.

"The same person who killed...?"

Burton shook his head.

"No, no, well, not directly, any way," he said. "She was trampled by a horse."

Tess looked at him in horror.

"I don't believe it," she said.

"The horse had been drugged. I guess he's normally a pretty gentle animal. We got the results back this afternoon on his feed and it'd been tampered with."

"Margo..."

"She's in the hospital. She's going to be okay, although Couple of broken bones. Ribs, arm. She's lucky. She never got hit in the head."

"'Lucky'."

"Well, you know. Hey, did you put a name in for a table?"

Tess nodded and they were silent for a moment.

"I was glad you called," she said.

"Yeah, well, as I said, I'm not sure why I did, and I gotta warn you, I'm not sure part of it's not official, you know?"

Tess smiled.

"Am I a suspect?"

"Everybody is at this point. Sorry. You're not very high up on the list if it's any comfort."

"Thanks, I guess it is, somewhat. Have you tracked down Jilly's ex?"

Burton nodded and signaled to the bartender to refill both of their drinks.

"Enough said about that the better," he said. "The man's an idiot. I don't know how he manages to live alone and care for himself."

Tess laughed.

"I think it's one of the things that appealed to Jilly. Mark's...I don't know, incompetence, I guess."

"Yeah, he's 'incompetent', all right."

"But he's sweet."

"I've seen the dearest old grandmas right after they've butchered their sons-in-law. Sweet doesn't cut much when it comes to homicides."

"I guess not. Is he higher up on the list than I am?"

"You could say so. Although I'd rather not talk about that little rat's ass tonight if it's all the same to you. Excuse the language."

Tess laughed again.

"Finding me colorful, are you?" Burton grinned at her.

"Very."

"I'm glad to see you're finally relaxing."

"You seem to have that affect on me."

"Not sure whether that's good or bad. In any case, it's probably the martinis."

"That's not very gentlemanly!"

"Hey, our table's ready. Come on." They picked up their drinks and Burton led the way to a private corner table.

"You ask for this, special?" he asked.

"No, I guess we just look like the clandestine-type."

"You mean 'sneaky'."

The waiter handed them their menus, took Burton's wine order and scurried away.

"I'm a married man and I'm not entirely sure why I'm here tonight." Burton spoke quietly, with no sign in his voice or manner of their earlier bantering.

Tess reached across the table and touched his hand.

"I do," she said.

Burton put down his menu and frowned.

"You do?"

She nodded.

Burton said nothing.

"I mean, the timing isn't great," she said, "--you're married and in the middle of a murder investigation--but that's how it happens. I don't think you get to pick when these things happen."

"You only get to decide what to do about them."

"God, you're going to think I'm depraved or immoral or something," Tess said, leaning back into her chair and spreading her napkin out on her lap.

"Why's that?"

"Because it never occurred to me that there was an option."

7

Tess let herself into the darkened apartment, and dropped her car keys on the hall table. She kicked off her Manolo Blahnik sandals and padded into the living room where she snapped on one lamp.

The evening had been tiring but exciting. She wondered, even after tonight, what he thought of her. She wondered if he doubted her attraction to him. He'd do well to, she thought. What a cliché! The sorority rich-bitch and the Sansabelt-Budweiser cop. Still, there was something there....She sank into the couch next to her phone machine and tucked her feet under her. My God, was there ever something there.

She snapped on the TV with the remote control and tuned to the local news station. She muted the volume and drowsily watched the gibbering news anchors. She picked up her cell phone from the coffee table. It showed three messages. Might he have called on his way home? she wondered. The kiss, surely, hadn't been a total surprise. After all, they'd touched hands, and in one case, feet, all through dinner. The parting in the moon-lit restaurant parking lot had been prolonged and intense. Kissing him had been practically *de rigeur.* She made a face. That wasn't it. She'd been longing to kiss those full, wry lips all evening.

What's gotten into me? Falling for the fucking homicide detective in a case that could send me to prison until I'm too old to care what I look like. Oh, Jilly, you bitch! Could you possibly have planned this, too? Somehow, it's got your ironic signature all over it.

The first message was from Portia: '*Oh! Tess! Did you hear about poor Margo? And to make it worse--*' and Tess fastforwarded through it. The second message was a hang-up.

The third was just one word, hissed out over the wires in a diseased gasp:

"Teeesssssss."

Tess jabbed the stop button and dropped her phone, feeling the terror swell in her breast.

It was him.

Chapter Five

1

The river birch trees had been planted so closely together that they now formed a long tunnel of dappled sunlight and shade on the dirt tractor-road that led from the main highway, past the pastures and riding trails, to the main barn and tack rooms.

Burton was surprised to see, growing along the bordering split-rail fencing, several mature lilac bushes. He'd remembered them from boyhood summer vacations in upstate New York and hadn't seen any since.

The late morning sun had burned off the dew from the jade-green pastures and he could see, as he and Kazmaroff rattled down the bumpy tractor-road, small groupings of grazing horses in both the pastures that lined the road. House finches lined the fence tops like a welcoming committee.

"Fucking peaceful, isn't it?" Kazmaroff said as he drove.

Burton didn't answer but surprised himself that he felt a small smile forming.

He'd tried not to think too much about last night. About The Kiss. He hadn't anticipated it; wasn't even sure how he felt about it. He knew it was taking a stronger will and discipline than he had ever exerted --including his attempt to quit a twenty-five year nicotine habit--not to analyze and examine the why of it and, more importantly, the what-next-of it.

"The barn manager's out of the hospital," Kazmaroff offered as he pulled the unmarked cruiser in front of the largest barn building.

"Whad'she have?"

"Broken ribs, broken arm. Few cuts and bruises."

Burton nodded.

He'd told Tess last night that he thought he and Kaz could be finished here today. It was impossible, of course. He looked around and saw two uniformed cops, standing by the tractor shed, drinking coffee.

"Get a report, will you?" He said to Kazmaroff, and then walked into the main barn.

Kazmaroff stared after him in surprise.

Burton entered the dark barn and immediately spotted the young girl, Jessie, as she hosed down one of the ponies in the shower bay.

"Hey, Detective Burton!" the girl called out cheerfully. "Any news on Margo?"

Burton approached the girl and watched her work for a few seconds. The pony was sudsed from mane to tail and stood quietly in the cross-ties, enduring her bath. Jessie scrubbed her with a brush, then took the hose and rinsed her thoroughly. Burton noticed she was as wet as the pony.

"She's out," he said. "Probably on her way home now."

"I still can't believe it was Traveler," Jessie said. "Even on drugs. That horse is practically comatose. Who do you think did it?"

Burton watched the barn sparrows flitting maniacally around the rafters of the barn.

"Sometimes if we concentrate on 'why', we come up with 'who'."

Jessie stood in the shower bay, holding the hose down where the stream ran over her rubber boots. "Wow," she said.

"The doc says the drug was fast-acting," Burton said. "When were the horses fed?"

"Same time every day," Jessie said, now shifting from one foot to the other. "Five o'clock."

"And you do the feeding?"

Jessie nodded.

"Unless it's my day off or something."

"'Or something?'"

Jessie cleared her throat.

"You know, I'm sick...or something."

"I see. Did you feed the horses the night Margo was attacked?"

"I did."

Jessie looked miserable.

The pony shook himself like a dog and the flying water made the girl jump.

"Oh! Rocket! You scared me!" Jessie dropped the hose and turned back to the pony. She turned off the water and disconnected the cross-ties from the pony's halter.

"Were there a lot of people around during feeding time?"

Eagerly, Jessie nodded.

"Zillions," she said. "People tend to be finishing up around then, or just getting off work and coming out for an early evening hack or ring-work or something, you know?" She waved an arm at the barn. "That is, until you guys cleared the place. Pretty peaceful, now."

Burton nodded. He leaned forward and patted the pony's wet muzzle.

"We don't think the person who drugged Traveler's food intended to hurt Traveler," he said. "We think the intention was to do exactly what happened." He paused. "Margo typically in her office in the evening?"

Jessie nodded.

"Yes, well, you see," he explained. "Even a little noise would likely send her running to investigate, and something that had to do with one of the horses being in trouble--"

"It's true!" Jessie said, leading the pony out of the shower stall. "Margo wouldn't be thinking of her own safety if one of the horses was in danger or hurt, or something."

"And somebody knew that."

"Everybody knew that," Jessie said, emphatically, throwing a large towel over her shoulder. "Everybody who knew Margo, knew she'd go into that stall or try to handle Traveler. Somebody tried to kill Margo!"

"And now we have to find out why someone would want to kill Margo."

Jessie nodded.

"And then we'll know who," she said.

Burton looked down the long aisle of empty stalls.

"Where is everyone?" he asked.

"If it's a nice day, we turn 'em out," she said. "Bring 'em back in for dinner."

"My men making it impossible to keep the barn running?"

"They don't interfere with the horses," Jessie said. "And with no riders here, there's not much to do."

"Miss the riders, do you?"

"Like hell!" Jessie laughed.

"What do you know about Jilly Travers?"

"She was a bitch."

"Ever have any run-ins with her?"

"Everybody out here had run-ins with her!" Jessie laughed again. "But no, aside from making fun of me to my face and behind my back, she pretty much ignored me."

"How about Portia Stephens? Nice lady?"

"I like her."

"Tess Andersen?"

Jessie shrugged.

"I guess she's a friend of Margo's, or something. She's not mean to me or anything. I'm not sure we've ever spoken."

"Isn't that unusual in a barn this size?"

"Not really. Anything Tess wants done for Wizard, she goes to Margo."

"Her 'friend'."

"I guess. And then Margo has me do it."

"Well, thank you, Jessie. I think we'll be out of your hair in another day or so. You in charge, with Margo gone?"

Jessie grinned.

"That's what the owners said. They called from Indianapolis--that's where they live, can you believe it? Own a beautiful piece of horse farm like this and live somewhere else?"

Burton looked up and saw Kazmaroff signaling to him from the mouth of the barn.

"Better get that pony in his jammies before he catches a cold," he said.

He left to the sound of her girlish giggles echoing through the rafters of the big, empty barn.

2

"Nothing," Dave said, when Burton joined him. They walked to the parking lot, the gravel crunching under their feet. "They've covered every inch of the barn areas and offices--"

"What about Margo Sherman's house?" Burton nodded toward the small one-story cottage tucked between a tractor shed and a large tack shed. Margo's car was parked out front.

Kazmaroff nodded.

"Nothing there," he said. "Smells like dried horse shit, but aside from that, nothing."

"The car, too?"

"Jesus, man." Kazmaroff looked away in exasperation. "Yeah, the car, too."

"How about the office?"

Kazmaroff shrugged.

"Dusted, photographed..."

"But that's it?"

"We didn't see a body, Jack," Dave said sarcastically.

"Good for you, Dave. Great detective work."

"Hey, Jessie!" Burton waved to the girl as she came out of the barn, leading the pony. She stopped.

"Which one is Traveler?"

Jessie squinted and pointed to a herd in the pasture beyond the tractor shed.

"The big bay in that group," she called. "Vet said he was okay now."

Kazmaroff frowned.

"Bay?" he said.

"Learn something," Burton said, pleasantly. "And Best-Boy?"

"Who the fuck is..."

"He's in the paddock. Jilly would never let us turn him out with the others." Jessie came closer.

"Why is that?"

She shrugged. "The horses beat up on all newcomers to the pasture, you know? Until everyone learns their place in the pecking order. Jilly didn't want to chance Best-Boy ending up with teeth marks on his butt or maybe missing an ear or something."

"A real animal lover, I guess?" Burton said.

"Oh, yeah, right," Jessie laughed. "That was Jilly all over! Anyway, you can't miss him, he's the only half-Clydesdale-Thoroughbred in the paddock."

"Big Mother," Kazmaroff said, looking in the direction of the paddock.

"You can say that again."

The two men walked over to the paddock. As soon as they were close, the sole horse in the paddock charged the fence.

"Jesus!" Kazmaroff yelled, jumping back.

The horse wheeled to a stop in front of the fence and snorted as if to say: *Hey! Where djya go?*

Burton approached the animal and put out a hand. The monster horse swung his massive head up wildly, then gently nuzzled the empty palm.

"Looking for a treat, big guy? Sorry." Burton scratched him between the ears and the horse dropped his head over the fence to afford Burton better access. "Somehow I can't imagine anybody taking a chomp out of *your* butt, eh?"

Kazmaroff slowly joined him.

"How big was Jilly?" he asked in awe.

"Five foot three," Burton answered. "I guess with Jilly it was all about size."

"Jesus. How did she get on him?"

"You know what I'm thinking, Dave?" Burton gave the big horse a final pat on the neck. "I'm thinking whoever killed Jilly in the clearing had to be involved with horses somehow."

"That's a real brainstorm."

Burton ignored his comment.

"Because anyone who wasn't familiar with horses would've been scared shitless to have approached her riding this monster."

Dave was silent.

"He seems gentle enough," he said finally.

"Oh, he is," Burton said, turning away. "He's just pent up. Not much room to run here." He handed Kazmaroff the car keys. "Why don't you see if you can scout up some lunch? I want to look through Miss Sherman's office a little more thoroughly."

Again, Burton walked off leaving Kazmaroff off-balance and more than a little peeved.

Before he disappeared into the main barn, Burton turned.

"And, hey, if you see Jessie on your way out, tell her to throw Best-Boy into the pasture with his buddies. I'll take the responsibility."

3

The gnarly little groundskeeper hunched over the worktable in his trailer and strung another large bulb of garlic onto the necklace. He tested the string for strength then put it on over his head and tucked it into his sweat-stained polo shirt.

The very thought of his date this evening made him wobble and he sat down hard on one of the torn dinette set chairs.

The police had talked to him two times now. Once after Jilly was killed, and once again after Margo was hurt by one of them horses. They thought he was an idiot. That was clear. Especially that big, fancy-dress cop. The jerk must have thought he was deaf too, because he heard the cop refer to him as 'the dim-wit.'

Oh, we weren't really so dim-witted as the world thought, now were we? Especially when we have so much more than all the other poor losers of the world.

He squeezed himself in a tight hug as if he could not possibly contain his glee.

4

"Yeah, well, I didn't want to wake you," Burton said in his phone.

"You knew I was awake." The voice was stern, defensive.

"Whatever." Burton glanced around Margo's office and let the silence build.

"Are you coming home tonight?"

"I'm home every night, Dana," Burton said with exasperation. "I had to work late *one* time in six months...and, Jesus, it's not like you need me for something. I'm sure all your favorite sit-coms will still continue to provide you--"

"I don't know why you're being so hateful. You should be glad I still care *when* you come home."

"Yeah, I guess it's a real barometer of the state of our marriage," Burton said. He stood and peered closely at the framed photograph on the wall of Margo and Jilly and Mark Travers. And Tess.

"Don't be sarcastic, please. Mother and Dad are coming for the weekend--"

"*This* weekend?"

Oh, Christ.

There was another silence.

"I'll see you when I see you," she finally said. And hung up.

Burton disconnected and returned to the picture on the wall. All the suspects and the victim in one tight little picture, he thought. He concentrated on Jilly first. She actually looked soft in the picture, vulnerable. Was there another side to her that hadn't yet been seen? And then Tess. God, she was beautiful. Ten years ago. Burton shook his head. Maybe Kaz was right and she *had* hedged her bets against the years with some cosmetic surgery. So what? He looked at the young Tess again.

It's gotta be hell to lose it once you've had it.

He noticed that she appeared unattached in the photograph. She was unattached now. An uncomfortable thought niggled at him. Come on, he chided himself.

It doesn't mean she's been available her whole life. Someone that beautiful...it wouldn't make sense.

The knock at the door made him jump.

Kazmaroff stood in the door way, a large McDonald's bag in his hand. Whatever pleasure Burton might have taken earlier in turning Dave Kazmaroff into a luncheon delivery boy was immediately replaced by the anxiety that Dave's smile triggered.

"Something up?" Burton asked, reaching into the bag Kazmaroff had deposited on Margo's desk.

"I didn't know what you wanted in the way of beverage," Dave said pleasantly. "So I didn't get you anything."

"What's up?" Burton repeated. "You heard something?"

"A little something," Dave said, reaching for his own burger.

Burton wondered how much of his pension, if any, he could still retain if he threw Kazmaroff through Margo's plate glass window overlooking the north holding paddock.

"Headquarters got Portia Stephen's deposition this morning."

Burton stopped in mid-bite.

"And?" he prompted.

"She changed her story, man."

Burton put his sandwich down and stared at his partner. He knew it was coming and now, strangely, he felt in no rush to hear it.

"She says she's sorry she forgot to tell us before," Kazmaroff continued. "But now she says it's only true that she and Tess Andersen left Jilly in the clearing..."

"What does she mean 'it's only true?'"

"She means, up to that point, it's true. Do you need extra catsup? It's *after* they left the clearing that her story changes...."

Burton said nothing. He stared at his hands and waited.

Kazmaroff took a large bite of his hamburger and spoke through a full mouthful:

"She said that Tess Andersen went back to the clearing alone."

Chapter Six

1

It didn't rain at the outdoor memorial service, which was slightly unusual for November in Georgia. Burton stood next to Kazmaroff and felt the sweat trickle down his neck. It was hot, which was also not usual for November.

The service was held on the polo grounds at Bon Chance Farm. Jilly's son, Justin had chosen the site, and while the motive behind the decision probably lay in some gruesome irony twisted up in young Justin's mind having to do with the site where his mother was savagely murdered, the rest of the service attendees chose to believe the site-choice was a tribute to his mother's love of riding.

The young man, himself, sat in the first row of folding chairs. He wore jeans, a navy gabardine blazer, Gucci loafers and no socks. And a nasty smirk across his pink cheeks. No one sat in the row with him. Behind him sat Mark Travers in dark chinos, a tan blazer and sunglasses. Burton could see Travers' flashing white caps even at forty yards distance.

He and Kazmaroff stood off to the side of the chairs, not easily visible by the mourners, but not hiding either. There was a coffin, even though there was no body. Burton wondered what was inside. Her saddle? Her whip? The severed head of a beloved childhood pet?

Next to Mark sat Margo, bandaged and doped. Burton noted she leaned heavily on Mark and that he held her hand. Burton and Kazmaroff exchanged a look.

Behind Mark and Margo sat Portia and her husband, then Tess, and Robert Shue, Jilly's boss from the agency. They were all dressed elegantly, somberly, and did not speak to each other. In the last row of chairs sat several people whom Burton recognized as boarders at the barn. He was surprised to see Kathy Sue there. She was holding the hand of a pudgy bald guy who looked like he should have a sign across his chest reading "Corporate Accountant". There was no sign of Lint or Jessie.

The Methodist minister approached the speakers stand that had been covered in carnations and spoke briefly, generically, about the sudden loss of life and the overall need to accept tragedy in one's daily round. Burton tuned him out and continued to survey the stand of mourners.

His eyes rested on Tess.

So. She had lied.

She looked away from the minister and found him. She smiled a small smile. He wasn't sure but he thought she winked at him. He felt his stomach clench.

"...and more to those left behind who need endure the terrible vacancy, the insurmountable..."

"It gives 'em both opportunity and motive, you know," Kazmaroff said under his breath.

Burton turned his focus back to Mark and Margo.

"Neither have alibis," he noted.

"One of 'em knows horses well enough not to be intimidated by a Clydesdale," Kazmaroff said. "Hell, she's nearly as big as Best-Boy, herself."

"Very nice, Dave."

They were silent a moment, then Burton spoke:

"Nothing draws people together like hating the same person."

"None of which eliminates Miss Andersen's involvement in this," Kazmaroff said pointedly. "She doesn't have an alibi either."

Justin Travers took the minister's place at the stand and stared out over the gathered crowd, a huge grin across his face. Burton noticed the boy's hands fidgeted a lot with the carnations.

"Good-bye, Jilly!" Justin said happily. "Good-bye, Mommy-sweetest. How we will all miss you. Thank-you, Reverend, you must surely have known my mother intimately to have been able to talk as you did just now."

Burton saw the minister flush angrily in his seat in the front row.

"Uh-oh," Kazmaroff said. But he was smiling.

"I, for one, will miss the daily, incessant phone calls," Justin continued. "The constant interest in even the smallest detail of my life--my grades, what tests I had coming up, have I met any nice friends? The woman was insatiable!" He leaned over the podium and pointed to Robert Shue. "But I guess you know that, huh, Mr. Shue?"

"Make a note to talk to Shue again," Burton said.

Robert Shue frowned fiercely at Justin and spoke a few words to Tess who appeared to nod sympathetically.

"Oh, yeah, and I'm sure Miss *Andersen* will be a willing ear to tell your troubles to!" Justin continued. "Isn't that right, Tessie? '*Come to Mama'*, huh?"

"Shut-up, Justin!" Tess spoke clearly above the murmurings of the crowd. "Say what you need to say about your poor mother and then sit down!"

"This is a joke!" Kazmaroff said, still obviously enjoying the joke.

"Well, I'd like to do just that right now, thanks," Justin said, the humor temporarily gone from his face. "Although it's nice to be told 'shut-up' in front of fifty people at your mother's funeral. I wish you could try it sometime--"

"You can't have it both ways, Justin," Tess shot back. "If you hated her, then save your spleen for another time. If you've got something nice to say about her--"

"Now YOU shut-up!" Justin screamed. "You hated her! So don't lecture me about how to behave! You fucking bitch, you probably killed her!"

Tess looked at him in horror as Mark jumped up and tried to calm the boy down. Justin twisted away from his ex-step father's attempts to soothe.

"And now I've got nobody!" he sobbed, surprising everybody. "I don't even have a poor excuse for a mother, I've got nothing because somebody got selfish or jealous or something petty and fucked, and now I've got nothing and nobody, and I hate you for it! I hate all of you!" Justin dashed from the podium, knocking over a huge display of flowers from Shue's agency. He stopped long enough to grab up a handful of dirt and pelt the casket with it.

"Just watch things here," Burton said to Kazmaroff. "I'm going after him."

Burton followed the boy, allowing him enough space to choose his retreat. Justin ran, without apparent design, down the dirt and gravel tractor-road, past Margo's house and the cars parked for the service in front of the main barn, and up a small incline to a wide gate which opened onto what was known as "the geldings'" pasture. He stopped at the gate and hung on it, hugging it to him. Burton gave him a moment and then began a purposefully noisy walk up the incline. Justin whirled around, his eyes blazing, his cheeks streaked with oily tears. He looked confused at first, as if he couldn't place Burton, then seemed too weary to process how he felt about him. He turned back away and let Burton walk up to him.

"Pretty wild, back there," Burton said as he draped one arm on the gate. He noticed that some of the horses -- ever in search of an unexpected carrot or apple chunk -- were starting to wander over to the fence. He easily spotted Best-Boy among them.

"Leave me alone," the boy said, not turning to face Burton. "Everyone just leave me the fuck alone." He buried his head in his arms and leaned against the gate. Burton thought the gasping sounds he heard from the boy were his desperate attempts not to weep. Suddenly, the boy jerked his head up, just as three horses from the herd -- Best-Boy among them -- edged in closer to the gate.

Justin screamed in surprise and fear and waved his arms at them. Burton fought the impulse to stop him from scaring off the horses. Hell, it might do him some good, he thought. The horses shied sharply, then wheeled away and galloped back to the herd, spraying pebbles and dirt clods behind them. Justin watched them go, his face streaked with tears.

He turned to look at Burton and Burton was careful not to show any indictment.

"It's okay," Burton said.

The boy put his head back into his arms. And this time, he cried.

2

Tess straightened the folds of her Ungaro jacket. It shimmered like liquid silver across her lap and she touched it as if she could gather solace or strength from its fabric. The heel of her Prada pump pushed into something soft on the dirty linoleum floor. Gum. She took a deep breath and tried to compose herself.

"Can I get you anything?" Burton asked. He didn't look at her when he made the offer. He and Kazmaroff sat with Tess and a female police officer in the small interrogation room. They'd intercepted her immediately after the memorial service which, thanks to Justin, had been cut short. Burton noted that Tess had revealed no surprise at being asked to return with them to headquarters for questioning. He wondered if Portia had confessed her changed deposition to Tess.

Tess shook her head.

"No, thank you," she said.

"Nice service for Jilly," Kazmaroff said idly. "After Justin's departure," he said to Burton, "some people actually got up and said some nice things about her."

"Why were you there?" Burton asked Tess.

Obviously flustered by the abruptness of the question, Tess refolded her jacket again.

"I...well, I...why wouldn't I be there?" she asked looking from Kazmaroff to Burton.

"You mean, seeing how you and Jilly were so close and all?" Kazmaroff asked.

Tess appealed to Burton.

"Should I have a lawyer here?" she asked.

"Probably," Burton replied, not looking at her.

"Oh, my God," she said, staring at him.

"Portia Stephens says you lied about leaving Jilly that afternoon," Kazmaroff said, leaning in close to her. "She said you told her to lie to the police about what really happened."

Tess licked her lips.

"I don't need a lawyer for this," she said. "It's all easily explainable."

Burton looked at her.

"Explain, please," he said.

"I did go back for a minute...and there was no sense in both Portia and me returning, so I told her to wait for me and I was going to go back and get Jilly--"

"Portia says you told her to return to the barn," Kazmaroff said.

"Well, that's untrue."

"Would you be willing to take a lie detector test?" Burton asked.

Tess looked at him, her eyes filled with pain.

"I...yes, of course," she said, softly.

"What happened when you went back?" Kazmaroff asked.

"Jilly wasn't there."

"Did it look like a chain-saw massacre had taken place?"

Tess gave Kazmaroff a disgusted look.

"It looked just as I'd left it not two minutes earlier."

"So, you mean, blood and human tissue were clinging to rock and trees?"

Tess stood up.

"Am I being arrested for murdering Jilly?" she asked, her voice shrill and shaking.

"Sit down, Tess," Burton said, tiredly.

"Yeah, sit down, Tess," Kazmaroff said, sarcastically. "We're not there yet."

"You didn't look for her? Call out for her?" Burton asked.

Tess sat back down. Her Ungaro jacket slipped to the floor.

"Of course, I did," she said, speaking only to Burton. "But I was having a problem with Wizard. He was acting really agitated, spooked. It was all I could do to keep him under control. I swear, I thought he was going to bolt on me."

"So, you...?" Kazmaroff prompted.

"I went back to rejoin Portia. Honestly, I didn't put it past Jilly to be hiding in the bushes trying to make my horse shy! It's the sort of sick, childish thing she would think of."

"How easy would that be, do you think?" Burton asked gently.

"What? Make my horse shy?"

"No, hide in the bushes with a 2,000-pound Clydesdale."

Tess opened her mouth to speak, then closed it.

"So," Kazmaroff prodded her. "You rejoined Portia on the trail?"

"No," Tess said quietly. "She'd already gone on ahead."

"Even though you told her to wait?" Burton asked.

Tess shook her head.

"I thought she understood me. Maybe she didn't."

"Yeah, I guess using the fact that Portia's not too bright and could've got your instructions wrong is as good a defense as any," Kazmaroff said.

Tess shot him a look filled with hatred.

"I did not give her instructions," she said.

"So you're saying Portia's not involved in this? You acted alone?"

Tess looked at Burton.

"I think we have more than enough for today," Kazmaroff said, smiling. "Thank you, Miss Andersen for answering our questions. You've been very cooperative," he added sarcastically.

"You're finished with me?" she asked Burton.

Burton just stared at her.

"Show Miss Andersen out," Kazmaroff said to the female police officer. "We don't have enough to hold you at present," he said to Tess, his voice sounding to Burton like a flat tape recording from one of his wife's sit coms. "We'll just have to ask you to be patient."

Tess snatched up her jacket and walked from the room, her left foot sticking to the floor with every stride.

3

The scratching sounds of the mice as they evacuated the open tack trunk made Margo turn her head in time to see the little beasts--their stubby tails like tiny apostrophes--scurry out the tack room door.

Where's that stupid cat? Margo thought as she eased herself down against an empty saddle rest. The pungent-sweet smell of leather mixed with the musky smell of oats and grain. The barn was silent except for the muffled crunchings of a dozen horses eating their morning Wheaties in their straw-padded stalls.

"Can you believe I'm riding him? Isn't it wild?"

Jessie stuck her head in the door and grinned at Margo, who blinked at her silhouette before the bright morning sun. Jessie stood, in schooling chaps and riding sneakers, next to Best-Boy. The strap of her riding helmet hung, unlatched, down her cheek.

The huge horse lowered his massive head and nuzzled Jessie's shoulder.

"It's like riding a building!" Jessie added, gleefully, scratching the animal between the eyes. "Aren't you, sweetie-pie?"

"Don't let him do that," Margo said, wincing as she tried to shift her weight on the saddle rest. "The last thing we need is a horse his size thinking he's boss."

Jessie held Best-Boy's stirrup and placed her foot in it.

"I need a step-ladder!" she yelped. Swiftly, she climbed into the saddle and adjusted her stirrups. She paused for a moment and looked at Margo, hunched over and broken, leaning against one of the saddle rests in the darkened barn. "You gonna be okay?" she asked.

Margo shifted painfully again and grimaced.

"Just make sure that horse is okay," she said, tartly. "Or you'll only be exercising Dancer and Puddle-Glum from now on." Margo surprised herself by her sharp tone.

"Oh, we'll be fine," Jessie said, turning the horse away from the barn. "Don't worry about us."

Tired of trying to get comfortable, Margo walked down the aisle of stalls, talking briefly to a horse or two. She stopped midway down the long walkway and put her hand out to the chestnut quarter horse eating noisily in his stall. The plaque outside the stall read "Beckett."

"Hey, boy," she said, softly. The horse swung his head away from his feed and moved instantly to the sound of her voice. Inexplicably, Margo felt tears spring to her eyes. *God, when was the last time I visited my own horse? Let alone, rode him?*

How long before she'd be able to again?

"Hey, boy. Don't got any sugar for you today, pal." The horse nuzzled her hand, his glossy brown eyes regarding her with sleepy affection.

Margo left the barn, watching Jessie and Best-Boy manage the gate to the south pasture. She must be going to take him on a trail ride, Margo thought with surprise. She had assumed the girl would exercise him in the ring. She watched Jessie latch the gate behind her without dismounting and then break into a trot toward the pasture and the woods beyond. Even at this distance, she could see the smile on Jessie's face. And the sight made her wonder the last time *she* had smiled just to be on horseback, the sun on her back, a dry trail before her.

She shook her head and slowly limped her way back to her office in the main barn.

I'm practically a suspect in a brutal murder, not to mention someone tried to kill me. I've got injuries--some of which will alter how I do things for the rest of my life--I'm in constant pain, and what am I thinking of? I'm wondering why the fun seems to have gone out of riding!

She laughed, then clutched her chestful of broken ribs.

As soon as she reached her office, the phone rang. She took her time maneuvering over to her desk to answer it.

"Hello?"

"Hey, Margo, sweetheart, is this a bad time?"

"No, Mark. I got lots of time." Margo eased herself into her desk chair, trying not to whimper onto the line as she did so.

"I was hoping to come by today. Maybe take you to get something to eat, what do you think?"

Margo closed her eyes and smiled sadly. How many years she had waited for this phone call, to hear those words.

"I can't," she said.

"Man, this is killing me," Mark said.

"I know."

"I mean, how does us seeing each other make one of us the killer?"

"It doesn't," she said. "It just doesn't help."

"But we need each other now."

I needed you before.

"I know, Mark."

"This just sucks. I want to help, Margo. You need someone to look after you."

"I'll be fine," she said, wincing again. "I've got Jessie."

"Oh, for craps sake--"

"Mark, it doesn't look good. It only throws suspicion on the both of us, now, please--"

"You mean, when it's all over and they've nabbed the killer...?"

"Yes...I..." Margo rubbed her eyes with a shaky hand. Had she taken that morning's pain medication? She couldn't remember. "Yes, of course, that would be great."

"You mean it? Because, honestly, Margo, I've always wanted to...you know. I've always felt it was you and me, you know?"

"Yeah, me, too, Mark, really," she said.

It's too late, it's too late.

"So, when it's over?"

"Yeah, that'd be good." A motion out of her large picture window caught her eye and Margo turned to see Jessie and Best-Boy galloping full-speed along the trees that lined the perimeter of the pasture. She could see Jessie's pony-tail streaming out behind her in a horizontal line, matching Best-Boy's big broom of a tail. Jessie looked like a little doll on the huge horse. Best-Boy looked so heavy and mammoth, yet he flew down the line of woods like Pegasus, his legs churning the air in powerful rhythm. As Margo watched, allowing Mark to become a blur of background noise, she suddenly found herself possessed by a strange and compelling joy.

Almost a revelation.

4

"You bitch! I can't believe you told them!"

Portia looked unhappy. She frowned at her husband as she spoke into the phone. *Can't you do something?* she seemed to say to him.

"Just hang up on her," her husband said, patting his pockets in search of something.

"They made me tell them," Portia said into the phone receiver.

"Did they also make you call up and ask to change your deposition you fucking traitor?!"

Portia looked at her husband again and this time he smiled and shook his head.

"Portia, hang up on her," he said. "Oh, here they are." He picked up his car keys and held them up for her to see.

"I'm not good at lying," Portia said into the receiver.

"Are you good at being friend-less?!"

Portia looked at her husband and frowned.

"She hung up on me," she said.

Her husband laughed and walked over to Portia and kissed her.

Tess slammed down the phone and whipped a large Lladro figurine to the floor in the next second.

"Bitch!" she screamed.

The phone rang. She snatched it up.

"I'll never forgive you, never! You deliberately made it look like I had something to do with Jilly's death!"

"Well, did you?"

Tess caught her breath so sharply she began coughing. Finally, she took a long breath. She sat down on the couch, her shoulders collapsing about her like an old woman's.

"I didn't kill Jilly," she said miserably.

"I don't think you did either," Burton said.

Tess lifted her head.

"Then why did you...why was I...?"

"That was standard, Tess. We got new information, we had to bring you downtown to flesh it out..."

"But you didn't even warn me! Just yanked me from the memorial service...I didn't even know...I was completely unprepared!"

"Telling the truth doesn't take much preparation."

"Oh, yes it does! It does when the truth, on the face of it, can be so easily misconstrued. You know it does!"

"I want to see you."

"Oh, Jack." Tess wanted to weep.

"I want to see you."

"Professionally?"

"That's inevitable, but no. That's not how I want to see you."

"When?"

"This evening? I thought we'd take a trail ride together."

"So, it's business."

"I told you, Tess, that's inevitable. But I don't think you killed Jilly and I do want to see you. So, what do you say?"

Tess paused.

"You can ride Beckett," she said. "Margo won't mind and he needs the exercise."

5

Kathy Sue pulled the hem of her jacket to drape more fully across her chubby knees. The two detectives sat in the flowered loveseat she and Ned had made love in that first night. She found herself looking around her own apartment, as if seeing it for the first time. She'd known they were coming; had known it from the moment she'd received word about Jilly's disappearance. She was ready for them.

"And so you worked closely with Jilly Travers?" The big, burly one asked her. Detective Kaz-azinsky, or something.

"The shop's not that big," she answered. "We all work closely together."

"Some of the other employees have said that you did not get along with Jilly," the other detective asked. She wondered if he was the boss of the two. He was good-looking in an older-guy kind of way.

"Who said that?" she asked with as much innocence and surprise as she could muster, considering she was starting to sweat between her thighs.

Kazmaroff flipped through his notebook. He looked up and smiled.

"Just about everybody," he said pleasantly.

"Well, I...no, I liked her okay," she said.

"Really?" Again, the big detective smiled at her.

"Well, I mean, we weren't best friends or anything," she said.

Shit! Where was Ned? He was supposed to be here with her for this!

"No, I guess not," the older guy said. "Especially since the rumor in the office is that your fiancé slept with Jilly a few months back."

Kathy Sue stared at the detective. Her knees gaped and she didn't try to pull her jacket down to cover them. She felt a distinct buzzing in her ears as the detectives continued to talk at her but she no longer heard the specific words.

One of them, the big guy, kept asking her something. His voice kept spiraling upward at the end of his sentence. Same sentence. Same spiral. Same question.

"....going to ask you, Miss Rappaport?"

Kathy Sue closed her eyes.

"I hated her," she said.

The room was quiet. Then,

"What happened, Miss Rappaport?"

"It's bullshit that Ned slept with her," Kathy Sue said. She looked at the big one. "It's the kind of nasty bullshit that she would have spread around the office, to try to hurt me, humiliate me. But it didn't happen."

"You admit you hated her."

"I was glad to hear she was dead."

"We don't know that she is, for sure," the Detective Kaz-guy said.

Kathy Sue saw the unkind look that the older guy gave his partner.

"Let's assume for our purposes that she is," the older guy said to her.

"I hope she is," Kathy Sue said.

Suddenly the door opened and a man, thirtyish, stood poised in the door frame. He was balding, short and pale. He was wearing jeans but gave the impression of being somehow formal and tailored. His eyes, behind round, John-Lennon spectacles, were probing and anxious.

"Kathy Sue?" he said.

"Oh, Ned, you're here!" Kathy Sue jumped up and folded herself into the young man's arms.

"I'm sorry I'm late, babe," Ned murmured. "Are these the guys?"

Burton stood up.

"You're Ned Potzak?" he asked.

Ned nodded and helped Kathy Sue back to her chair.

"That's right," he said, seating himself next to her.

"You ever sleep with Jilly Travers?"

Kathy Sue shook her head vehemently, but watched her fiancé.

Ned looked astonished. He looked from one detective to the other.

"I never even met the lady!" he said.

Kathy Sue let out a long, agonized breath.

"So, the answer is no?" Kazmaroff asked him.

"No, I never slept with her."

"I told you!" Kathy Sue said. She clutched Ned's arm and he patted her knee.

Kazmaroff turned to Kathy Sue.

"Where were you at three o'clock last Wednesday afternoon?"

Kathy Sue opened her mouth and looked unhappily at her fiancé.

"I was home, sick," she said.

"Can anyone verify that?" Burton asked.

Kathy Sue shook her head.

"I can verify it!" Ned said.

"Oh, Ned..." Kathy Sue said unhappily.

"I talked to her half the afternoon," he said.

Burton turned to Kazmaroff.

"Check the phone records, see if anyone was talking to anyone around three o'clock."

"I'm almost sure I did," Ned said.

"Oh, Ned," Kathy Sue said. She looked at the detectives. "I napped most of the afternoon."

Kazmaroff closed his notebook and stood up to stretch his legs. Slowly, Burton did the same.

"Not good," he said.

6

Tess cinched the girth and gave it a tug. Her long blonde hair was plaited in back with the ends folded in a bun at the nape of her neck. Golden tendrils framed her face. She wore a simple navy-blue cotton sweater over dark jodhpurs and black riding boots to her knees. Burton thought she looked stunning.

"Let's be wild tonight and ride hatless," she said, handing him the reins of his mount.

"Suits me," he said. They'd arrived in separate cars at just before seven in the evening. The days were much shorter now, but the full moon would allow them plenty of light for their hack.

"Beckett's a sweetheart," she said, swinging up onto her appaloosa. "You'll love him. He's very responsive. Not a pig like this guy." She patted her horse lovingly on the neck. "How much riding did you say you've done?"

Burton faced the horse and gripped the saddle. He slipped his foot into the stirrup and swung effortlessly into the saddle. Beckett waited patiently at a standstill.

"Enough," he said. "Although never in an English saddle. It's like riding bareback."

Tess laughed, and Burton thought this was the first time he'd seen her relaxed.

"Come on," she said. "Let's see what the moonlight looks like on the Chattahoochee."

"You've got a trail along the river? Is it the same one you and Jilly took last week?"

Tess walked her horse in front of Burton for a moment without answering.

"Is that where you want to go?" she asked, finally.

"Not necessarily."

"Good."

Burton trotted up alongside her. The two rode through a large fenced cow pasture, careful to avoid a group of muddy bovine eyeing them suspiciously, and entered a copse of trees on the other side of the pasture. Burton pointed out a trio of sandhill cranes to Tess as they flew overhead.

He watched her eyes as she studied the birds and appeared to appreciate the rarity of their appearance. Out here, she didn't seem any less poised to him, but there was a relaxed quality to her body, her facial expression, a naturalness that he hadn't seen in her before. As he watched her scratch her horse between its ears with her riding crop, he found himself thinking Tess was the most unexpected concoction of society maven and tomboy. A whole different type of person he had no idea existed.

Or perhaps existed only in Tess?

"So, tell me," he said. "What's the point of all this?" They were stopped on the trail, deciding between a fork of two paths, one that would take them along the river and one that wound deeper into the woods. "I mean, grown women, giving up their precious time and money to jog around in circles on horseback? What's the attraction?"

Tess grinned at him.

"You really don't know?"

"Ah, now, don't give me that domination theory stuff...the idea of holding something big and powerful between your knees that you women can control..."

"I hate to spoil the ultimate male fantasy for you!" Tess laughed.

"Well, then, what?"

Tess shrugged and leaned down and patted her horse again.

"There's no one answer, Jack," she said softly. "It's about love, mostly."

"Like the love of golf? Or the Braves? That kind of love?"

Tess made a face.

"No, it's about friendship kind of love. Come on, let's ride along the river. It's pretty in the moonlight.

"This horse has seen some incredible sunsets with me. He's carried me over fences that are taller than I am. We once galloped down a hill so fast, my head was resting on his butt the whole way...I thought we'd *both* be going home in bodybags...how can I explain? We've done brave things together, scary things. Very intimate and tender things. When life sucks, I come out here and ride with Wizard and I'm transformed. He does that for me."

"There's an argument to be made that golf could do that for you, too."

"*Golf?*" Tess shook her head. "I also feed him, clean out his not-so-little footies, brush him all over, sponge-bathe him, baby-talk to him, outfit him in the most expensive leather goodies, scratch him in all his favorite spots--"

"Hold on, I'm starting to feel threatened here."

Tess laughed and leaned over and touched Burton on his jacket sleeve.

"It's damn near like that!" She said. "I've got married friends whose husbands are jealous of their wives' horses. I'm serious!"

"I can see it."

"Oh, no." Tess shook her head at him. "I can't imagine you all insecure and stupid like that. Impossible."

Burton enjoyed the brief touch of her hand on his arm.

"What about you?" she asked. "Got a hobby when you're not arresting the bad guys?"

"It's funny," Burton said. "I totally forgot about something I used to love as a kid. And since I've had to be out at Bon Chance, it's come back to me."

"You're not going to say tractor-pulls, are you?"

Burton laughed.

"Oh, I wish I'd thought of that! No, it's birding. I used to be obsessed with it when I was a boy."

Tess smiled.

"Birding? You mean, bird-watching? Really? You know all their names?"

"Yeah, I do. I really do. Isn't that wild? My Dad and I were really into it together. We were passionate about it."

"Your father still alive?"

"Nah. He passed away about ten years ago. My mother's still kicking, though."

"Any brothers and sisters?"

Burton grinned at her.

"This is the full dossier-part of the relationship, I guess."

"Only I suppose you don't need to ask me the same kind of questions."

"I've had the benefit of police computers," he admitted. "I learned your background the boring way, not the saunter-down-the-bridle-path-in-the-moonlight-way. My loss."

"Brothers and sisters?"

"One of each. We're fairly close. I was raised in Cocoa Beach, and my family is still there."

"Wow. You grew up with the moon launches?"

"Yeah, my old man worked at the Cape. He was the safety engineer on all the Apollo launches. We got to see a lot of them close up. It was fairly cool."

"It must have been paradise growing up right on the ocean, with everything going on that was happening back then."

Burton looked at her to see if she was teasing him. She didn't seem to be.

"It was," he said. "I was lucky."

"And how is it you came to be a cop?"

"That is another long and boring story," he answered. "For another time. And the whoa-ing part of the program is still done by pulling back on the reins?" he asked.

"You want to stop?"

"Just checking out my equipment."

"Yes, just pull back. And sit, sort of down into Beckett's back, too."

"You mean as opposed to how I'm sitting sort of not down on his back right now?"

Tess laughed.

"It's a little different. Guess I'd make a bad teacher. I can't explain it."

"Maybe instinct will take over," Burton said. He leaned over and kissed Tess on the mouth. Whether by unconscious command or willing accomplice, their mounts stopped for the duration of the kiss. When Burton pulled away, Tess continued to rest her hand on his thigh. The natural light had died but the moon illuminated the path before them.

"I've fallen in love with you, Jack."

"It's only fair."

"What are we going to do?"

"We'll do whatever is natural and right."

"I'm afraid those are contradictory issues for us."

Jack smiled and brushed aside one of Tess' loose curls.

"Don't worry about it, little girl," he said softly. "Don't worry about anything right now." They kissed again. Burton clenched his knees tightly into the horse to keep from falling off.

The rest of the ride was slow and pleasant. The unseasonable heat of the day had dissolved into a cool, autumnal evening. The flies were long gone and the mosquitoes were hanging out down by the pasture pond. Burton and Tess rode in single-file along the Chattahoochee, each with their own thoughts, watching the moon draw long jiggling trails in its black surface.

Later, as they were untacking their mounts in the main barn, they heard loud voices coming from Margo's office.

Burton raised an eyebrow at Tess, who shrugged.

"I haven't seen her since she's been out of the hospital," Tess said, scraping packed dirt out of her appaloosa's hoof.

"Not even to stop in and say hello?"

"We're not friends, Jack," Tess said a little too emphatically.

"No one's asking you to loan her your hairbrush, Tess," Jack said. "I'm wondering why you're over-reacting."

"*Me,* over-reacting?" Tess dropped Wizard's foot and reached for another.

"Yeah, any normal boarder would pop in and see how she's doing. You are making a point of not doing that."

Tess finished scraping out the hoof and eased it back to the ground.

"I'm avoiding her," she said.

"That's why they call me a detective," Burton said, still listening to the raised voices coming from Margo's office.

Tess grinned.

"And a damned good one, too," she said. "Don't ask me why."

"Why I'm a good detective or why you're avoiding her?"

Suddenly the door to Margo's office flung open and Margo hobbled out of it.

"Just get out!" she screamed. "Get out before I throw you out with my bare hands!"

An instant later, Justin Travers appeared in the doorway, brandishing what looked like a large club over his head. He swung the club wildly, chipping away splinters of wood from the door jamb directly over Margo's head.

"I will kill you!" he screamed at her, raising the club once more. "I will kill all of you!"

Chapter Seven

1

Justin froze in position as he watched Burton dash up to him and snatch away the polo mallet. Without thinking, Burton smacked the boy against the head with the flat of his hand, dropping him to the dirt floor of the barn with a hard thud. Justin sat there, dazed.

Burton turned to Margo and held her by the elbow.

"Miss Sherman?" he said, giving her a gentle shake. "How you doin'? Let's go in and sit down, huh?"

Tess took Margo's other arm and the three of them stepped over Justin in the doorway and returned to Margo's office.

"Don't even *think* of going anywhere," Burton said to him.

They settled Margo in her chair and Tess rummaged in the book shelves for a bottle of water.

"She always keeps water in here," she murmured. Finding the bottle, she uncapped it and held it to Margo's lips.

Margo stared at Tess, her eyes filling with tears.

"Oh, Tess..." she started, weakly.

"Oh, stop it, Margo," Tess said without conviction. "Drink this and tell us what happened."

Justin stood in the door, his right cheek red with Burton's slap. Burton gave him a sharp look and Justin scowled down at his own feet.

"So, what happened?" Burton repeated.

"He wants Best-Boy destroyed," Margo said, her voice rising shrilly. "The little bastard wants to kill Jilly's horse! Says he's got authority to--"

"And I do, too!" Justin shouted. "She left everything to me, so he's mine to do what I--"

"Shut-up, kid," Burton said. He turned back to Margo, who was openly weeping now, and allowing Tess to hold her. "I'd be happy to drag his little ass downtown if you want to press charges, Miss Sherman." He looked back at Justin, who jerked his head up at Burton's words.

"Oh, Jack," Tess looked at Justin and frowned. "Do you think that's necessary? I mean they were both just upset about--"

"That's up to Margo," Burton said.

"No, no, no charges," Margo said. "Unless he tries to move Best-Boy! Then I will! You can't have him! Detective, he can't take him, can he?"

"I have no idea," Jack sighed. He looked at Tess and they shared a sad smile. *Some ending to the night, huh?* he telegraphed. She nodded. *What did we expect?*

"Come on, asshole," he said to Justin. "Let me finish brushing down the horses and I'll drive you back to your barracks. Where'd you get the alcohol, anyway?"

Justin blushed angrily but didn't speak.

"Yeah, never mind." Jack touched Margo's shoulder. "You gonna be okay here?" She nodded and looked at Tess.

"I'll hang around awhile," Tess said to him.

"Okay, good." He pushed to his feet. "Listen, I enjoyed the ride."

"Yeah, me, too," she said, her voice tired and sad.

"Come on, Justin," he said. "And I'll show you what horse-shit looks like when it's not falling out of your mouth. Sorry, ladies."

Tess smiled and shook her head.

2

"I hate that horse!" Justin whined in the car ride home. "She spent more time with that stupid animal than--"

"Oh, shut-up about the fucking horse," Jack said. "Why did you come to the barn tonight? Threats over the phone not convenient enough for you?"

"I...I wanted to tell Margo, personally."

"Weren't thinking about killing the horse yourself, were you?"

"Are you serious?" Justin blinked. "It's as big as Godzilla. I'd be afraid to touch it."

"You're acting like an idiot."

"Maybe I'm in mourning," the boy said, unsuccessfully fighting back tears. "Have you ever thought of that?"

Burton couldn't help laughing.

"Yeah, maybe you are," he said, watching the boy huddled up on the passenger side door handle. He felt a flood of pity for the kid, but there was something else too. The more time he spent with him, Burton got the feeling that underneath it all, Justin wasn't really such a pain in the ass as he tried to prove.

"It's hard to lose a parent," Burton said.

"I don't have anybody!" Justin whined.

"Yeah, and I'm saying that's rough." Burton turned into the parking lot of a local restaurant. He parked the car and turned in his seat to face the boy. "But you can decide to make it just as bad as it can be," he said. "Or you can decide not to let it turn you into the kind of nasty little shit nobody wants to have anything to do with."

Justin stared straight ahead through the windshield. The unspoken words hung in the air between them.

Like your mother.

"There's all kinds of reasons why people turn into assholes," Burton continued. "Believe me, sooner or later, I see 'em all. There's a whole jail-full of people downtown who had bad shit happen to them. And I mean really bad shit. But they're still in jail. Their life sucks just as bad, and in fact, worse, because of how they decided to handle their misfortunes."

"I won't end up a felon, if that's what you're thinking," Justin muttered.

"Glad to hear it," Burton said. He opened his car door. "Now let's concentrate on not ending up a dick-head, too. You hungry?"

Jack pulled off his shirt and threw it into a corner of the room. His wife lay immobile but awake in the Queen-sized bed. He sat on the edge of the bed in his Dockers and socks and looked out the small bedroom window to the spaghetti tangle of electric and telephone lines spun out between the utility poles in his yard.

After he'd dropped Justin off, Jack had checked in briefly to his office and then come home. Now, as he sat in the dark on the edge of the bed, he tried to remember if he'd eaten dinner. He didn't feel hungry. He slipped out of his pants and was pulling off his socks when his cell rang. Quickly, he picked up, glancing over at his wife. He noticed that there was no sound of deep breathing that might signal she was asleep.

"Yeah?" he said into the phone.

"It's me," said Kazmaroff.

Burton waited.

"One of the art directors at the agency says he overheard Kathy Sue Rappaport threaten to kill Jilly the day before she disappeared."

"Yeah, okay," Burton said. "Bring her in." He paused. "Is that all?"

"Unless you have something you want to tell me."

Burton disconnected, then slipped into bed next to his wife, careful not to touch her.

3

"I didn't do it! I wanted her dead, but I didn't do it!" Kathy Sue sobbed noisily into her folded arms on top of the table in the interrogation room.

Kazmaroff looked at his notes.

"This guy, Mike, at your office says you told him you were going to kill Jilly..."

"I never said that!" Kathy Sue jerked her red, wet face up and shouted at Kazmaroff. She'd only been in the room for fifteen minutes; she looked like she'd spent the night there. "He misunderstood me!"

Still looking at his notes, Kazmaroff said: "He said: 'She told me she was gonna put out the bitch's lights for good--'"

"He made it up! I'd no more say something so stupid and...trite...than walk naked down Peachtree. 'Put out her lights!' Can't you see he made it up?"

"Why would he do that, Miss Rappaport?"

"I don't know!" Kathy Sue looked around the room as if expecting someone to back her up. "Where's Ned? Has he called?"

"So you're saying you never threatened to kill Jilly Travers?"

"Well, God! I might have said...you know, 'I'd like to kill the bitch' or something like that, but people say that kind of thing, you know? It doesn't mean I was going to kill her!"

Kathy Sue deposited her red face back into her folded arms and Kazmaroff sighed and left the room. Burton stood outside in the hall, smoking.

"I thought you gave those things up," Kazmaroff said.

"She's denying it, of course," Burton said, dusting ashes off the front of his shirt.

Kazmaroff said nothing.

"Let her go," Burton said. "We can always pick her up later if something more substantial crops up. Meanwhile, the Chief wants to see us."

The Chief was not happy.

The owners of La Bon Chance Farms wanted the last of the police off their property, they wanted some confirmation that future riders would not discover a partially-decomposed body in the middle of a pleasant afternoon's ride, and they wanted all boarders to have unlimited access to the riding facilities again.

The Chief wanted a body. Dragged across and deposited upon his desk before the end of the upcoming weekend or both Burton and Kazmaroff would be doing drug busts for the rest of their uninspired, lackluster careers.

Kazmaroff wanted a new partner.

Burton wanted a new life.

4

"You know how sorry I am."

"Forget it, Portia," Tess said. "It's all out in the open now. And it's fine."

"So you really like this detective, huh?"

Tess pulled the saddle off her horse and watched the steam rise off his back. It had been a good, fast hack; the kind she liked best, cantering and galloping across the fields of stumpy grass, jumping the coops down by the east pasture. She felt positively weak-kneed.

"He's gorgeous," Tess said simply.

"You in love with him?"

"I think so, yes."

"That's so cool. Especially the part about his partner wanting to stick you with the murder and him needing to clear your name and all."

Tess shook her head.

"You're one of a kind, Portia," she said good-naturedly.

When would she see him again? Did he really know everything about her from the basic computer print-out one could discover on anyone living in this country, she wondered? Sure, he knew how she got her money and how she paid her mortgage, what stocks and bonds she had and what her last ten tax returns were. But did he know she was an Air Force brat and had traveled the world with her parents as a child? Would he be surprised to know she played in crumbling castles and bombed-out houses in post-war Germany as a girl, and, with her friends, dragged home undetonated bombs and grenades from World War II? Did he know she was more comfortable in riding clothes and blue jeans than Versace? Was he beginning to really know her? Would he get a chance to?

Tess sponged off the saddle area on her horse, watching the dirt stream down his sides in wet rivulets. Portia brushed her own horse's tail placidly.

"And you know, Tess. I never said a word about, you know...the other thing. The guy that was with you and Jilly in the clearing?"

Tess froze.

"What are you talking about?" she said, her words stunted and breathless.

"I heard his voice, Tess. I heard the guy you were talking to with Jilly."

Tess turned and stared at Portia, then felt a sudden and desperate need to run to the barn bathroom.

5

They drove in silence to the advertising agency of Ryan, Davis & Shue in the Atlanta Financial Center. Kazmaroff flashed his badge at the receptionist.

His favorite part of the job, Burton thought.

They stood in the waiting room which was lined with trophies and plaques of presumably successful advertising campaigns for presumably satisfied clients.

"Detective Burton?" Robert Shue entered the waiting room and stuck out his hand to Burton. He was dressed in an Armani jacket over tight jeans. A piggy little pony-tail in the back did little to vampire attention away from his receding hairline in front. His eyes were piercing and active, his handshake soft and friendly. Burton had the distinct impression he was being given the valued-client-treatment.

"We'd like to ask you a few questions," Burton said. His voice was flat, intentionally giving no indication as to whether Shue's charms were effective.

"About Jilly. Of course, of course. In my office. Zukie? Hold my calls, please. Unless it's my wife, of course."

Of course, thought Burton. It's important to let the fuzz know what a priority family is.

Shue ushered them into a large corner office. The desk faced an expansive window which looked out over Peachtree Road. Shue indicated they were to sit in a cozy seating arrangement of two color-coordinated loveseats bookending a large glass coffee table.

"We'll sit in our brainstorming corner, I think," Shue said as they seated themselves. "Can I get you anything to drink? I think I--"

"How long were you sleeping with Jilly Travers, Mr. Shue?" Burton asked.

"I...uh..." Shue involuntarily looked at the large leather-framed portrait on his desk of a pretty woman and a little girl.

"Your family?" Kazmaroff said, picking up the picture frame to get a closer look. "Nice people. How old's your kid?"

"Uh,...that was taken...uh..."

"Dates would be good," Burton said. "When the affair began...when it ended."

"*If* it ended," Kazmaroff said as he replaced the photograph.

"Good point," Burton said. "*Had* it ended, Mr. Shue? Before Jilly was killed? Or did her getting killed...end it?"

"I...we....oh, Christ."

"Take your time, sir," Burton said, easing back into the plush cushions on the sofa. "In fact, why don't we use this time to do a little brainstorming?"

6

Shue watched the policemen from his window as they walked to the parking lot. He'd had no idea the interview would be so threatening, so uncomfortable. The two of them worked him like they could read his mind.

Just when he started to think the big detective was sympathetic to him, he'd asked him how many other employees he had slept with! Who was he talking about? Zukie? Kathy Sue? Maybe Catherine? God, Catherine had to be fifty years old with more hair on her top lip than her head. And when he'd protested, the other cop, the bastard! asked if he also screwed clients! Christ! And then that stupid bitch on the front desk rang through with a call from his fucking wife in the middle of it! Is the bitch totally stupid?

He turned away from the window and stared down at the picture that Kazmaroff had handled earlier. He picked it up and gently eased out the smaller photograph tucked behind the displayed one. Jilly grinned at him malevolently. Her hands held her tits out to the photographer like she was offering him a deal on mangoes. Her pubic hair was hazy, out of focus, against her pale, peach skin.

Am I going to be able to pull this off? Or am I already dead?

7

"Did you get Travers in?" Burton asked as they drove down Peachtree Road away from Buckhead and the Financial Center.

Kazmaroff nodded.

"They said he squawked the whole way downtown. He's been coolin' his heels in a room for the last hour."

"Let 'im wait," Burton said. "Want lunch?"

Kazmaroff looked at him.

"You mean, as in, sit-down-with-you-lunch?" he said, "Or as in drop me off at Wendy's drive-thru while you go off and do something meaningful?"

Burton ignored him.

"Yeah, I could eat," Kazmaroff said.

Burton pulled the car up to a sandwich shop curb.

"Nothing for me, thanks," he said. "I'll pick you up in an hour."

"Fuck you, man."

Burton drove away.

8

"I hate this."

"Yeah, me, too." Burton peeled back the corner on a little plastic cup of creamer. He smiled at Tess as if to belie his words.

"Are we dating? Is this a something?" She asked, not smiling back at him.

"You know it is."

The noise of the fast-food restaurant picked up.

"I used to live at McDonald's as a kid," Burton said, musing. "If I wasn't eating here, I was working here."

"Really."

"Is something wrong, Tess? You seem a little quiet today. Margo was okay last night, wasn't she?"

"Oh, fine. No, I'm just a little tired is all. Tell me more about when you were a kid in Florida. That's a dream come true to us Yankees, you know."

"Not much to tell," Burton said, obviously winding up for a story. "As kids, we were always aware that where we lived was a tourist place, you know? And this was even before Disney showed up. My brother and I used to fish off this little bridge not far from the beach and our house, and we'd sell what we caught to the tourists."

"That's enterprising."

"That's one word for it. We'd sell 'em a fish called whitey because they always looked so nice and fat. They were nice and fat because they were full of worms."

"Ugh."

Burton laughed.

"My brother's a photographer down there now, living the freelance life. I'm not sure he's not still selling whitey to the tourists."

"Are you thinking of leaving your wife, Jack?"

Burton pushed his uneaten hamburger away. She looked so beautiful, he thought. Sitting here in an effin' McDonalds, her food in a styrofoam tub, dabbing her designer blouse with a paper napkin. He thought they must look like the rich bitch and her lawn man nailing down prices for the coming season.

"I guess I'm thinking about it," he said, slowly, watching her.

Tess smiled as if it hurt her to do it.

"Would it be because of me?" she asked.

"No, of course not," he lied.

"Tell me it hasn't been much of a marriage for a long time."

Jack leaned across the table and touched her perfect, unlined face. Dana's eyes had little baglets under them, the price of being forty-three and conscientious, he thought, about everything but her looks. Tess's plastic surgeon must have been good.

"It hasn't been much for a long time," he said.

"I love you, Jack."

"Let's just get through this week," he said. "Let me just handle one thing at a time."

"Can I help?"

"You could, you know."

"How. Tell me. I want us to get to the other side of this Jilly mess."

"Take me down the trail the three of you went last week."

Tess looked away. Jack imagined she was picturing that last ride with Jilly, remembering the weather, the mood, the anger.

"Yes, all right," she said, finally.

"I want to take Best-Boy down the trail again," he said.

She looked at him sadly and nodded.

"You can probably handle him," she said.

"It never occurred to me I couldn't."

9

Burton and Kazmaroff walked into the interrogation room that held Mark Travers. Travers jumped to his feet when the door opened.

"Not even a phone call! I've been here nearly three hours! Am I under arrest? Not even a glass of water!"

Burton came in and dropped a McDonald's Kiddie Meal onto the table in front of Travers.

"Ask Sgt. Owens to get Mr. Travers a glass of water, would you, Dave?"

"Sure, Jack. No problem," Kazmaroff said, exiting the door.

"Brought you a little something to eat, Mark," Burton said. "Go on, help yourself. There's even a toy in there."

"Look, you gotta tell me why I'm here. Have you found out something or has someone said something? Because it's a lie if they have! I didn't kill Jilly!"

Kazmaroff entered with a plastic tumbler of water.

"Yes, well," he said. "It's still a serious no-no these days to contract to have someone killed. Even if the killer is mentally retarded, as I guess yours was and not able to complete the assignment. That water's not too cold for you, is it? Sometimes the water here at the station is so cold, it really bothers my teeth. Do you have sensitive teeth, Mark?"

"Oh, I wouldn't worry about him, Dave," Burton said. "He doesn't really look like the sensitive-type. But yes, Detective Kazmaroff is absolutely correct, Mark. You have already admitted to a felony...that's what we call breaking a rule that's really bad...a felony. So you're probably going to be coming down here a lot and...in the end...we might decide to keep you."

"In fact, I'd say we probably will, don't you, Jack?"

"Yes, yes, I guess now that you mention it," Burton sighed and looked into the hamburger bag. "We probably will. I think these fries are getting cold, Mark."

"What the fuck do you want?" Travers looked like he would break down and begin weeping.

"Well, we have a question for you," Kazmaroff said.

"Yes," Burton said. "We wanted to know if you knew what Jilly's maiden name was."

"Are you serious?"

"Yes, it seems nobody can agree. We don't know what her name was prior to marrying you. Sort of silly, huh?" Kazmaroff giggled.

"It was...she was called 'Waynis'."

"What do you mean 'was called'? Like a stage name? Was Jilly a stripper or something before you married her?" Burton frowned as if in thought.

"No, no! Of course not! Her name was Waynis. That's all!"

"Besides, what kind of a dumb stage name would 'Waynis' be?" Kazmaroff chided his partner.

"You're right," Burton said. "Okay, thanks, Mark, for clearing that up. You can go."

"That's it?" Mark stared at them with his mouth open.

"Yep, that's it," Kazmaroff said. "Until next time."

10

Burton snapped on his desk lamp in the empty squad room. He glanced at his watch. It was after 8 p.m. Dana would be pissed. He hadn't called.

Kazmaroff walked up to his desk and placed his hands on his hips. It was an aggressive stance; Burton braced himself.

"Good interview," Kazmaroff said. "He's definitely upset."

"Yeah," Burton said, not looking at him. "So far, it's the best part of the case--harassing the little twerp."

"But you don't really think he's involved."

Burton looked up at him.

"He might be," he said.

"Yeah, Jack," Kazmaroff said. "And so might Annie the office cleaning lady, but it's not likely."

Jack didn't respond. He moved some papers around on his desk.

Now what? Why's the bastard hovering over me? If he's got something to say--

"I put in for a transfer," Kazmaroff said.

Burton stared at him.

"You're moving?" he said.

"No, man," Kazmaroff said. "I'm not moving out of the city. I asked to be placed with another partner."

Burton made a grunt of disgust but his mind whirled.

Isn't this good? Isn't this what I want? It's good, isn't it?

"What did the Chief say?" he asked.

Now it was Kazmaroff's turn to act disgusted.

"He said we had a great track record together, can you believe it? The bastard sits on our necks for four fucking years about what screw-ups we are, and then tells me we're his prime partnership!"

"You didn't know that?"

"That we're the best?" Kazmaroff shook his head. "No, man. I thought feeling miserable all the time was like some indication of how well we were doing. I mean, if you hate your job, and everyone tells you how much you suck, then, how can you feel like you're doing good?"

"You hate your job?"

"I guess I just hate working with you. I don't know about the job."

Burton nodded and pushed another stack of papers around.

"So did he say he'd do it? The Chief?"

Kazmaroff turned and walked to the door.

"He said he'd okay it if you agreed to it. I told him that'd be no problem." Without waiting for a response, Kazmaroff walked out the door, shutting it hard behind him.

Burton sat quietly at his desk, staring at the closed door of the squad room.

Finally free of the obnoxious son of a bitch.

He turned to pick up the phone to call Tess and confirm tomorrow evening's ride, when the phone rang.

It was his wife.

"I'm just on my way home," he said.

"Don't bother," she said. Her voice tired and unemotional. "Daddy called and Aunt Liv is worse. I'm flying down there tonight. I'm walking out the door right now. I left you a note and a casserole in the freezer."

"Sorry to hear about Aunt Liv," Burton said, his mind whirling with possibilities--none of them related to the old woman's condition.

"Yeah, right. So I'll be home Sunday night. I'll call you from the airport."

"Okay, yeah, I'll pick you up."

"There's my taxi. Bye, Jack."

"Bye, Dana. See you Sunday."

Jack hung up the phone. Times like these he almost regretted that he and Dana had never gotten into the habit of endearments. It would make things so much easier, so much less obvious. An interjected *dear* or *darling* could soften even the hardest circumstances, he thought.

He turned in his chair and stared at the telephone.

First Dave. Then Dana. Well, well.

Chapter Eight

1

The noise from the living room could be heard from the street. The sound of squealing children, mixed with an incessantly loony musical rift, forced Robert Shue to hesitate on the doorstep of his own home.

They'd obviously started early, he thought, wondering if the crowd of parked cars on the street front was a true testimony to the size of the crowd inside. *Sandra must have invited everyone in Chelsea's second grade class.*

"Daddy! Daddy! You're home early!" An exuberant little girl, her brown curls long and flying around her face, jerked open the heavy front door and flew into Shue's arms. He dropped his briefcase--even the one with the new laptop in it--and scooped up his daughter.

"Yes, of course, angel," Shue said, still holding the girl, and shutting the door behind him. "Had to see this kind of bedlam with my own eyes. Are you having fun?"

"Oh, so much fun!" The girl wriggled free and dashed off into the crowd of children.

His wife appeared in the doorway of the kitchen.

"Oh, good," she said, smiling. "The cavalry has arrived."

"Where are the parents?" Shue asked before kissing his wife on the mouth. "Are all these little darlings drop-offs? I thought the invitation read--"

"It did and they are." His wife laughed. "You know the line: 'Can I just dash down the street to...I won't be a minute and so-and-so's very well-behaved..."

Shue shrugged out of his jacket and threw it on the back of a kitchen chair.

"How many we got?"

"About twenty. Come into the kitchen and let's do a drink before we have to cut the cake."

"Chelsea's loving it," Shue said, watching his blindfolded daughter grab the end of the donkey's tail and jab it in the vicinity of the living room drapes.

"Oh, yeah, she's having a good time. How was work?"

Shue settled on a chair in the kitchen.

"Fine, fine. You look gorgeous, babe."

"Do I?" His wife grinned and swung her medium-length bronze hair around her shoulders. "You know how birthdays always make me try a little harder." She laughed. The sound made Shue feel like smiling. As soon as he did, he felt his stomach knot.

He'd met Sandra in college. Then, like now, she was sweet, energetic, loving, and rich. He'd loved her in spite of her being rich, or maybe because of it; he was never really sure. Sandra was just so *pleasant*, he reasoned when he married her. So if he *was* marrying her for her money, he'd decided, it was not at all disagreeable. Could be love, he thought, as he watched her now. It wasn't an easy thing to determine. It wasn't like how he felt about his daughter, for example. Now *that* was unmistakable and perfect. That was love in anyone's book. But if what he felt for his wife *was* love --and he dearly hoped that it was -- it was kind of like being friends, only you screwed.

He watched her as she made the gin and tonics, the sounds of their daughter's glee in the background, and considered the extreme lengths he would go to protect them.

2

Burton stood at the gate to the back pasture and squinted out across the field. Two blue jays bathed in a shallow mud puddle. He watched them as they splashed and ruffled their feathers.

Burton had purposely arrived early for the ride. He found himself savoring the time before Tess arrived, enjoying the anticipation. He hadn't yet told her about his wife's departure. He was savoring that, too.

Jack watched as one of the geldings nudged another one in the rump and the two seemed locked in a comraderly cuddle for a moment. Then, standing sleepily butt to head, each alternately administered an occasional lash of the tail to the other's face, shooing away flies and gnats. Jack smiled and shook his head, noticing other pairs in the pasture with the same cooperative arrangement.

"Amazing, isn't it?"

He turned to face Margo.

She hobbled up to the gate and used her arm not in a sling to pull herself up onto the first fence slat.

"They bat the flies off each other," she said, still staring out to the pasture of mares and geldings. "And if one of them hears something and freaks--that's enough for all of them to freak, too, and they'll all stampede. They're not a very independent bunch, horses."

"How you feeling, Margo?"

Margo eased herself back to the ground and stood next to Burton. She nodded.

"Better. I'm doing better," she said. "I've slowed down and it's good. I mean, I feel like shit and I'm afraid you think I killed Jilly and want to put me in jail, but aside from that, it's weird--I've never been better." She didn't look at Burton. "You're riding Best-Boy this afternoon?"

He nodded.

"With Tess, again," she said.

"That's right."

"Yeah, well, you should be okay. He's a little less excitable since he's been out to pasture."

"Have you ever ridden him?"

"Best-Boy?" Margo finally looked at Burton. She grinned. "No way. I mean, I'd love to. He's a fantastic horse, but..."

"But Jilly wouldn't have allowed it."

"You must think she was a real horror. She wasn't. Not really. I probably could've ridden Best-Boy if I'd pushed it. Hell, for that matter, I don't remember asking."

"You ever ride with Jilly?"

Margo made a face but whether from the question or her injuries, Burton couldn't tell.

"Years ago," she said.

"What happened?"

"You mean, why didn't we still pal around and ride together? Well, mainly, I took this job. It's one thing to hack with a friend who's also on the circuit and doing respectably in the ribbons-department, you know? It's a totally other thing if that friend turns into the barn manager at your boarding farm."

"Jilly was a snob."

Margo snorted a laugh.

"Yeah, I guess you could say that." She shot Burton a look. "No more of a snob than Tess," she said. "Maybe I shouldn't fault either of them for it. Maybe they can't help it."

"You sound angry."

"Oh, wow. You are so insightful." Margo began to hobble away. "You want a cup of coffee or something? Jessie's here. She can tack up Best-Boy for you before Tess comes."

Burton followed her.

"I didn't hate her," Margo said as they walked. "I couldn't hate her."

"And that would be because why?" Burton tossed a pebble into a squat of azaleas bordering the main barn.

"Mostly because I was in love with her," Margo said. Her back disappeared into the darkness of the barn.

3

The sun was beginning to set over the metal top of the commuter train tunnel. It burnished the slick silver top a contrasting orange, and reflected back up into the sage-green sky, sick with pollution.

Kazmaroff stood in the parking lot of the rail station, his cell phone in his hand. The station had been cleared of commuters and now only the homicide squad of photographers, police agent and junior detectives remained.

"Can you tell how long?" he asked the white-jacketed agent on his knees before him.

"Give me a break, man."

Kazmaroff grunted in impatience. He barked at a junior policeman. "Move the crowd back another twenty yards! They're trampling the scene." He punched in Burton's number again and listened to the recording explain yet again that his party was not available.

He snapped it shut, and turned his attention back to the police agent and the broken body in front of them.

The call had come in from dispatch about thirty minutes earlier:

"I think we got your body, Dave."

"Great! Where?"

"Oddest place. Stuffed in the trunk of a car at the Lindbergh MARTA rail station."

"I'm on my way."

Now, as he stood in front of the opened trunk of the late-model red Infiniti, he felt his guts turn. The smell was pretty bad already. Could be from the heat. Things didn't keep in this heat.

"Can you at least tell me if she was strangled or bludgeoned? I'm seeing blood everywhere. Could she have been strangled *and* bludgeoned? Is that a puncture wound?"

The agent looked at Kazmaroff with what appeared to be an attempt at patience.

"Five minutes, Detective. Just give me five minutes to collect the more fragile samples."

Kazmaroff squatted painfully next to the man.

"Don't touch her," the agent said.

Kazmaroff ignored him. He moved the mane of long hair away from her face to examine her neck. Angry red welts were visible.

"Enough to kill her?" he asked, pointing to the welts. "Or just part of the overall struggle?"

The agent made a noise of exasperation.

Kazmaroff leaned forward and extricated a strand of hay from the corpse's cotton sweater.

"Detective!"

"Yeah, man, I know," Kazmaroff said, standing again. "Don't touch."

He held the piece of hay in his fingers.

4

"You, bastard! You killed her and I've spent the better part of the week in jail for it!"

"Don't be ridiculous, Kathy Sue," Shue said, shifting the phone to his other ear and closing the door to the den. "They've only questioned you this week--"

"I'm going to tell them what I know! I'm going to tell them what I saw!"

Shue felt his stomach muscles contract. His eyes fell on a silver-plated frame of a photograph of his family at Hilton Head last summer. Chelsea looked so little. Sandra, so beautiful.

"What, exactly, is it you think you saw?" he asked quietly.

"The company car," Kathy Sue hissed. "You used the company car! I had to get the office lap top out of the trunk..."

Shue saw in his mind the mud-encrusted shoes. Saw the gaping trunk, the blanket, the empty wine bottle...

"...Jesus, there was even a map to Bon Chance! I looked everywhere for the murder weapon. Where'd you hide it? Was it in with the tire jack?"

"You shouldn't believe everything you--" he began.

"Oh, give it a rest! It's over, Bob! I'm calling Burton and Kazmaroff tonight! You bastard! You were going to let them hang *me* for it!"

"I didn't kill her, you stupid girl!" Shue whispered harshly into the phone, his eyes on the door to the den. "I was fucking her. Are you so far removed from that sort of thing you can't see it when it's displayed in front of you?"

"I...uh..."

"We had a rendezvous, you idiot. At the barn. Did you see the blanket? The wine bottle? I was having an affair with Jilly."

"But, I...the map..." Kathy Sue whimpered.

"Tell a single soul what you saw and you can forget copywriting...I'll see to it you never get a job *proof-reading* in this business, do you understand? Make trouble for me and my family...falsely accuse me...and I'll hurt you in ways you cannot imagine. Are your fingerprints on the company car now?"

"Well, I had to get the laptop out of the--" Kathy Sue was nearly in tears.

"I think we understand each other."

Shue hung up the phone.

5

Margo pointed to the image of Mark Travers in the group picture on the wall of her office.

"We were together then."

"I thought he was married to Jilly at the time."

"That's true."

"Jilly ever find out?"

Margo eased herself into her desk chair.

"No."

"So you were in love with Mark Travers as well?"

Burton reached for his coffee; instant, in a chipped mug with the words 'I'd rather be riding' imprinted on it.

"I thought so at the time. Truth is, he was using me to get back at Jilly."

"Rather ineffectively if she didn't know about it," Burton observed, still scrutinizing the photograph.

"Yeah, well. He certainly didn't have the balls to let her know about it. I think it was an internal thing with him. You know, 'She treats me rotten, but the joke's on her' kind of thing."

"Man's a moron."

Margo laughed involuntarily.

"Yeah, I guess he is. I cannot imagine he had the spine to kill her, though."

Burton shrugged.

"We'll see." He turned to Margo and set his cup on her cluttered desk. "So, you are bisexual?"

Margo made a face.

"I don't know what I am. I know I loved her. I know that much. You're not getting a complete picture of her, Detective. She wasn't a monster. She had depth and--"

"Did she love you back?"

Margo sighed.

"In her way," she said.

"In that non-monster like way of hers."

"You've made up your mind about her, haven't you?"

Burton picked up a horseshoe paperweight and put it back down.

"I'm still making up my mind," he said.

"I tell you, she was too complicated to be defined in just one way. There was much more to Jilly than the fact that she could be cruel."

The phone rang. Margo picked up, said a few words and handed it over to Burton.

"It's for you," she said.

"Burton, here," he said into the mouthpiece.

"Finally." Kazmaroff's voice crackled over the phone line. "Jack, we got a body down here at the Lindbergh rail station. I been trying to get a hold of you for the last hour."

"What the hell's it doing at an in-town train station? Have the docs examined it yet? How'd you find it?"

"We got an anonymous call."

"Get Travers in to I.D. her," Jack said. He picked up a pencil and tapped the desk with it. From Margo's office, he could see the parking area for the barn. He scanned the lot for Tess's car. "We'll be able to shake him up again while we're at it."

"I don't think Travers would qualify as next of kin, Jack."

"What are you talking about? You're not thinking of getting Justin to come down--"

"Look, man, I'm sorry, okay?"

Burton could hear the tightness in his partner's voice. He dropped the pencil on the table, his eyes continuing to search the parking lot outside. Burton had the impression that he had stepped outside the scene and was now standing on the perimeter, watching. Waiting.

"...wasn't Jilly, Jack. We thought so too at first. This really sucks, Jack. You got to come down here. It's Tess."

Chapter Nine

1

Kazmaroff picked up his notebook and stared at his handwriting on the page. He glanced at the clock in the squad room. It was a little after ten p.m. Jack should be back from the morgue any minute.

He put his hand on the telephone, debating about whether or not to call and cancel his late date or try to make it.

Burton had been controlled and cold when he arrived at the murder scene.

So what else is new?

But he'd been somewhat vacuous at the same time. After Jack had ID'd the body and questioned the police agent, Kazmaroff had had to remind him where he'd parked his car when it was time to follow the body down to the morgue. He'd actually found himself feeling something--what? sympathy?--for the old bastard.

Suddenly, the door to the squad room swung open and Burton walked in. He looked at Kazmaroff as if he didn't recognize him.

"You still here? Thought you had plans tonight."

Had he mentioned his date? He must have.

"You okay?" Kazmaroff hadn't intended to say it, surprised himself when it came out of his mouth.

Burton seemed to tense up but his reply was noncombative enough.

"Like you said, it sucks."

"I'm sorry, man."

"Anything else come in?" Jack remained standing, as if he intended to leave quickly.

Kazmaroff stood up and snapped off his light.

"The copywriter at Jilly's agency called."

"Kathy Sue."

"Yeah, she accused Robert Shue of killing Jilly. Said she found the murder weapon in his car."

"You check it out?"

"As we speak. We can talk to her tomorrow. She'll keep."

Burton cleared his throat. Kazmaroff suddenly found himself intensely uncomfortable in the squad room. He began to envision himself out the door, down the stairs, and racing toward his patiently-waiting date in his car.

"Anything on tonight's murder?" The words were mumbled.

"No, man. We got the tip. Male voice, about where to find her. The coroner says she was..." Kazmaroff hesitated.

"It's okay," Burton said, smiling woodenly. "They told me the important bits. Strangled, but not to death. Finished off with a heavy blunt object."

"Yeah, well, that's about all I know."

"She was supposed to meet me at the barn tonight."

Kazmaroff nodded. He hadn't known. He wasn't surprised.

"Doc says she was killed sometime yesterday," Dave said.

"I couldn't reach her yesterday," Jack said.

No one could've.

"I'm taking off now," Dave said.

"Yeah, me, too. I'll walk out with you." Burton snapped off the overhead light. The two walked silently to the parking lot and parted without another word.

2

The next morning they questioned Kathy Sue at her apartment.

"I told you it wasn't me," she said as she let them in. "You saw the stuff in his trunk? I'm not surprised he killed her. They were having an affair, you know."

Burton and Kazmaroff moved into the living room but didn't sit.

"We're checking it out, Miss Rappaport," Kazmaroff said.

"The map? Did you see the map? And the muddy boots?"

"Who's in the kitchen?" Burton asked, still standing.

Kathy Sue snatched up a pack of cigarettes from the coffee table.

"Well, this should end it, right? Have you arrested him?" She asked.

Burton moved to the kitchen and motioned for Ned to join them in the living room.

"I was just bringing coffee, officers," Ned said, carrying a tray of steaming mugs in his hands. Burton thought the man looked edgy. Hard to tell the reason for it. He and Kazmaroff just naturally made people nervous.

"We've got a few more questions," Kazmaroff said, peering out of the living room window.

"Questions?" Kathy Sue smoked and looked from detective to detective. "You've got your man--"

"We have another murder, Miss Rappaport," Burton said, tightly, "that we believe is connected to the first, and for whom Mr. Shue has an alibi."

"I don't believe it!" Kathy Sue looked bewildered.

"Where were you yesterday afternoon from one to six p.m.?" Kazmaroff studied his notebook as he spoke.

Kathy Sue looked helplessly at her fiancé.

"In a client meeting," she said, finally. "Downtown." She stubbed out her cigarette in disgust. "Shue was in it, too. Is that his alibi? *Me?"*

"You and the nine other people in the meeting," Burton said. "We'd like to ask your fiancé a few questions."

Kathy Sue snapped her head up.

"What for? About me?"

"With you or without you," Kazmaroff said, his impatience beginning to show. He got eye contact with Ned. "It's your call."

Ned set his coffee mug down and picked up Kathy Sue's hand.

"Babe?" he said. "Let me have a minute with the detectives. Nothing's going to happen," he said, waving away the beginning of her objections. "You go on upstairs and finish getting ready and I'll see them out. You're a bundle of nerves, sweetheart.

"Here, take your ciggies..." He handed her the pack of cigarettes and pulled her to her feet. "Go on, honey. Let Ned handle it, okay?"

Kathy Sue gave the policemen one last, distrustful look and began to walk out of the room.

"I don't care where the bastard was yesterday afternoon," she said. "I know he killed Jilly. I know he did."

The men in the living room waited while she climbed the stairs. Burton remained standing. Kazmaroff sat and took a sip from one of the coffee mugs.

"Hey, this is good," he said.

"Colombian roast," Ned said. "I grind it myself."

"How long were you sleeping with Jilly?" Dave asked.

Ned didn't answer. He picked up his own coffee mug but didn't drink. The silence grew among them.

Finally:

"It was just the one time," he said, staring into his coffee.

"Does your fiancé know?"

"I confessed everything."

"I thought Jilly Travers was such a nasty slime-bag?"

Ned shook his head.

"She was." He looked at Kazmaroff as if expecting more sympathy from his direction. "She was also very seductive."

"She seduced you?"

"I take full responsibility for my behavior," Ned said firmly. "Kathy Sue has forgiven me and it's in the past."

"How recently in the past is it, Mr. Potzak?" Burton spoke quietly.

"Months ago," Ned said. "Maybe five months ago."

Kazmaroff stood up.

"And your own where-abouts yesterday?"

Ned licked his lips.

"I was at work," he said.

The detectives moved to the front door.

"Then you don't have anything to worry about," Burton said.

3

Burton got into the passenger side of the car, surprising Kazmaroff. He buckled himself in and stared straight ahead through the windshield.

"What do you think?" Kazmaroff asked as he started the car up.

Burton shrugged. They drove in silence for a few miles.

"Check out his alibi."

"Obviously."

"I'm going back to the barn."

Kazmaroff frowned.

"What for?"

"I'm going to retrace the route of the ride that the three women took when Jilly disappeared."

"We did that, man."

"Not from horseback."

"You're going to...?" Kazmaroff accelerated on the entrance ramp to Georgia 400. "You want company?"

Burton turned and looked at his partner.

"You ever been on a horse?"

"Everyone's been on a horse."

"Not these kind of horses. They're not as understanding as the rent-a-ponies at the amusement parks. I'd end up carting you back in a make-shift stretcher."

"It's nice to know I wouldn't be left on the trail."

Burton looked at Kazmaroff.

Is something happening here? Dave was behaving a lot less obnoxiously these days.

The thought sort of made him nauseated.

"Just drop me at my place," Jack said. "I need to pick up a few things."

"We've never talked about...you know...Tess."

"What's there to say?"

"Well, for one, like, why was she killed? Who did it? How is it connected to Jilly's murder?"

"It's connected."

"I think so, too," Kazmaroff said. "If the same person killed Tess that killed Jilly, then maybe Jilly was killed for a totally different reason than just being the biggest bitch on earth."

"The thought occurred to me."

"So, who did they know in common? And what were they into?"

"I think the key is the horses," Burton said.

"But that just doesn't make sense," Dave said. "How could a horse--unless it was a triple million dollar stud or something--be the cause of two violent murders?"

"Don't forget Margo," Jack said. "She was nearly killed herself. All three attacks are connected to the barn."

"Maybe we should get her some protection."

"That's a good idea. Do it, will you? This is my exit." Burton pointed to the exit ramp.

"What about Shue? We did find lots of interesting evidence that he'd been to Bon Chance."

"Dave, he was screwing Jilly; naturally he'd been at Bon Chance. On the basis of the evidence we found in his trunk, we'd have to suspect any one of forty boarders at the barn. We didn't find a murder weapon, did we?"

"You know we didn't."

"We need to have Travers picked up," Burton said.

Kazmaroff picked up his cell phone and tossed it into Burton's lap.

"Police harassment or a warrant this time?" he asked.

Burton picked up the phone, trying to decide how he felt about how it got there, and finally punched in the number for HQ.

"We don't have to decide right away," he said.

4

He hadn't slept the night before.

Dana had called from Florida and seemed surprised to find him there. The conversation had been brief and, although pleasant, unpleasurable for both of them. She would stay in Florida through Thanksgiving.

Jack tossed his Dockers onto the bed and pulled on the jeans he usually wore to work in the yard. November had finally shown itself with a bite in the air this morning that hadn't dissolved as the day continued. He pulled on a clean sweatshirt and made himself a pot of coffee.

Outside on the back deck, he stood drinking the coffee, observing the birds in his back yard. He watched the nuthatches bob along the ground, looking for something to peck at, and heard the big old pileated woodpecker drill into the far side of the dead sourwood tree at the middle of his yard. He watched the tree closely to catch a glimpse of the showy woodpecker.

She must have seen something, he thought. She must have seen the murderer when she went back to the clearing. He took a long, scalding sip of his coffee.

And possibly the murder itself.

The woodpecker peeked from around the tree looking like a segment from a Woody Woodpecker cartoon. He disappeared again and began his rat-a-tat-tatting noise even more loudly.

If she was killed because she saw Jilly's killer, then she kept quiet about it because she *knew* Jilly's killer. For some reason, she hadn't felt endangered by him. Burton forced an image of Travers to mind. It just seemed so unlikely to him that that wimp could have killed two women with his bare hands.

A rose-breasted grosbeak performed a touch-and-go on the chain-link fence Burton shared with his neighbor, then disappeared into the tree branches.

If she wasn't killed because of something she knew or saw, then the second murder could only mean one thing:

They had a serial killer on their hands.

Burton tossed the dregs of his coffee into a bush below his deck and put the mug down on the old, splintered picnic table on the deck. He waited for the woodpecker to reveal itself again. The bird was still thumping wildly away; the sound seeming to reverberate in the morning air, like a mini-construction crew at work in the back yard.

This was no serial killer. Her murder was a clean-up murder. A messy detail tidied up from the first murder. She had seen too much; and now she would never be able to speak too much. The pileated woodpecker flapped noisily away, and Burton watched him settle onto the roof of his neighbor's split-level. The jack hammering began again.

Was it only Monday when he had seen the sandhill cranes? When he had pointed out their lovely flight to Tess?

Tess.

The name came to him in a slow, snaking rhythm of pain and hunger. He sat down hard on the edge of one of the picnic table benches with the sheer force of it.

My God, how could I have lost you?

Jack covered his face with his hands.

5

Portia loaded her brush with ochre and touched it delicately to a piece of paper towel to disperse some of the color. She studied the sky on her paper, waiting for the azure-blue to dry just a bit more before adding the yellow. Too much too soon would spoil it all. Finally, she added the brush stroke of dull yellow and watched the colors mingle and meld in the winter sky. She snatched up a clean brush and held it, poised, over the paper in case corrections were needed. But no, the colors were getting along just fine. A smile came to her lips as she watched her painting.

"Ms. Stephens?"

Portia held her smile and looked up. Her maid stood in the doorway to the sun room, a load of pressed shirts in her arms.

"Yes, Juanita?"

"There's a policeman to see you."

6

Margo hung up the phone. She looked around her office, her eyes resting on the group photograph, picking out Tess from the crowd. She stared at it for a few seconds, then hoisted herself to her feet and hobbled to the door.

"Jessie?" she called.

"Yes ma'am?" The reply was cheery, nearby.

"Stop calling me that, you little shit, and go get Best-Boy tacked up. Western saddle, long stirrups. He's going for a ride."

7

An hour later, Jack stood in the darkened, late- afternoon barn. The sun filtered in through the wooden slats overhead, making brief oblongs of bright light dance and jiggle on the sawdust floor. The mourning doves cooed and waddled the ground outside.

He walked down the center aisle of stalls until he came to the stall of Tess's appaloosa. He paused, noticing the plaque that read "Wizard. T. Andersen." The horse moved from the back of his stall and jutted his face out over the gate. Jack put his hand up and instantly the horse nuzzled it, nickering softly.

"He'll miss her, too," Margo said as she walked down the aisle behind her. "I saw you drive up. Just takes me awhile to do the meet-and-greet these days."

"You needn't have bothered," Jack said, without turning around.

"He's a real sweetie," Margo said, patting the appaloosa's neck. "One of the best in the barn. You could ride him, if you'd rather."

"No, I don't think so."

"He's real gentle--"

"Is Best-Boy ready?" Jack turned away from the stall and faced Margo.

"Yeah, sure. He's up at the upper barn."

"Look," Jack said, running his hand through his hair. "I'm sorry. I know you loved her. I'm sorry..."

"It's okay," Margo said. "You loved her, too."

For a moment, the two stood in the quiet barn, listening to the sounds of the sparrows in the rafters and the mice in the tack trunks.

"Come on," Jack said, finally, walking away. "Let's do it."

8

Jessie stood quietly, holding the mammoth horse's reins in one fist, watching Margo and Burton approach.

"Okay, boy," she said quietly to the horse. "Just a little bit longer now." She nodded to the pair as they got closer.

"Hey, Detective," she said. "He's all ready for you."

"Thanks, Jessie," Jack said, eyeing the huge animal.

"Bill said a part of the fence is down along the western pasture," she said to Margo.

"Bill?" Jack patted Best-Boy's neck and checked the girth to make sure it was tight. The horse seemed wired. Very alert and energetic. Burton hoped he could handle him after all.

"Bill Lint," Margo said, patting the horse's rump. "He's an idiot but helpful. He's the groundsman for the polo field," she added.

"Yeah, and he stinks, too," Jessie giggled. "He eats garlic all the time and you can smell him over the dung and the horses from about a mile away."

"Anyway," Margo said to Burton. "Just be mindful that there's a gap there, and take it slowly. There's some spots on the trail that take concentration."

"Tess said she and Portia and Jilly took the whole ride at a trot," he said.

"I'm sure she did," Margo said, shaking her head. "Told you that. Anyway, who knows? Maybe they did. Jilly and Tess are...were great riders, and Portia has no sense. Maybe they did. Just watch what you're doing."

"And this baby, here, doesn't like water," Jessie added. "You'll need to push him over the creek."

Burton imagined himself, on the ground -- hands on the monster's large rump -- pushing him across a creek bed.

As if reading his mind, Margo leaned forward and pulled out a small crop from Best-Boy's saddle.

"Just give him a couple taps with his behind the girth." She placed her hand on the animal's lower flank. "And let him feel your heels at the same time. He'll cross the water. No problem."

"Why the Western saddle?" Jack asked.

"Safer. You don't mind? It won't affect the ride or what you see along the way."

Jack gathered the horse's reins in one hand, positioned his foot in the stirrup and swung up into the saddle.

"Once you get past the first fork after the polo field, just follow the trail," Margo said. "You'll be fine."

Jack touched his hand to an imaginary cap in salute, and turned the horse away from them.

"He'll be fine," Margo repeated as she watched him go.

Jessie turned and gave her an odd look.

9

Burton walked Best-Boy out the open gate to the pasture and slowly, down the fence line of the pasture. He felt his legs alongside the huge animal's sides and tried to relax, blowing air out through his mouth. Best-Boy felt bouncy and energetic under him, and Burton found himself wondering when he had last been exercised. Maybe Margo was right and Wizard had been the more sensible choice? He gripped the reins tightly, then reminded himself to relax. Maybe Dancer?

Before long, the pasture brought him to the choice of two paths and he turned down the one to his right. Immediately the trail began to narrow, with foliage and bushes crowding in closer.

Burton urged Best-Boy down the narrow trail, cringing in spite of himself at the leering branches of the bordering poplars and sycamores. They raked his jacket and jeans as he passed.

Had the three women really chosen this path for a pleasure ride? It looked, if not impassable, at the very least, unpleasant. Further to his right, the trail plunged down into an ugly ravine of rocks and trail garbage--trash bags, a discarded washing machine, and a few soft drink cups, their straws still jutting out of the lids like tiny exclamation points. He kept his eyes directed between his horse's ears, afraid to influence the beast's sense of balance by leaning over. A misplaced foot in this shiny mud would bring them both down the twenty foot drop. An image of the two thousand-pound animal landing on him came unhappily to mind.

It was annoying to Burton, rather than reassuring, that his horse seemed unaware that this trail was something less comfortable or safe than any other. Best-Boy responded to Burton's riding commands--a light thigh squeeze, a tentative touch of heel to flank--with begrudging but resigned obedience. Nonetheless, the detective felt grateful for the security of the big western saddle. It straddled the Clydesdale's back like an awkward yet comfy easy chair.

The limbs of the shrubs and saplings reached out from both sides of the trail, at varying heights, to inhibit his progress. As he trudged through the congestion of limbs, Burton gripped the reins tightly in one hand and pushed the more aggressive branches back with the other.

Suddenly, the tunnel of branches ended and he came upon the bank of a small, muddy creek, which separated him from a glowing opening of sunlight and space: the clearing where the murder had occurred. The gelding shook his head and slowed to a stop as Burton sank his spine stiffly into the saddle.

He thought of the nerve-wracking trail he'd just escaped. He had walked it at a slow gait. Tess and Portia had reported that they and Travers had taken it at a brisk trot. After the argument, the two had left a furious and unrepentant Jilly to return to the stable. One by one--first Portia and then Tess--they had retraced their steps back to the home barn. An hour later, Best-boy had returned, riderless, to the barn.

Jack squeezed with his thighs, pushing the horse forward into the water. He forced himself to stay relaxed. Best-Boy picked his way daintily across the little stream without any hesitation. He seemed eager to reach the other side, however, and scrambled up the small, sloping far bank, surprising Jack and nearly unseating him. They left the creek behind and stepped into the clearing.

He had been here many times before, of course, but had never seen it from this height. He walked its perimeter on Best-Boy, looking through the trees. He spotted a bald eagle and moments later, an indigo bunting. He didn't bother studying the ground--so far below him. It had been thoroughly searched and examined by his men.

He sat in the middle of the clearing, recreating the murder in his mind, trying to fix where Jilly and Tess had stood arguing on horseback. As the afternoon waned, so did the warmth from the sun. He pulled his blue-jean jacket close around his throat and pointed the horse back to the creek.

A feeling began to niggle in the back of his mind when he turned Best-Boy around for the return trip to the barn. He let the feeling alone, neither shaking it away or attempting to drag it front and center. It would explain itself in due course. Instead, he turned around in the saddle and imagined, yet again, Jilly and Best-Boy standing in the clearing next to Zanzibar and Portia, Wizard and Tess. Jilly would've been higher than the other two, of course. Himself, he felt agitated, yet relieved, after the harrowing pleasure trail, but the three experienced riders would be feeling...what? Exhilarated? Bored? Nothing?

They were arguing among themselves, he reminded himself. Or at least Jilly and Tess were. He developed a picture of Portia sitting primly on her gelding, staring happily at the

Georgia pines rimming the clearing while her companions exchanged insults.

Tess...

Burton felt his stomach clench. He saw her in his mind's eye, her golden hair streaming out from under her black velvet rider's hat. Another part of him, the Detective, knew she would've had it pinned up or tied back, but he insisted on the other image. He saw her face frowning at Jilly while she kept Wizard on a short rein, perhaps prancing in agitation around Best-Boy while the two riders argued.

Doesn't her own murder absolve her? he found himself wondering.

She couldn't have done it. She fought with Jilly, yes. She lied to me out of fear and insecurity. But then someone killed her...*the same someone who...*

Burton shook his head in an attempt to banish the thoughts. It was no good. He wasn't thinking clearly. He wasn't trying to learn something new here. He was trying to set up evidence for a theory he already believed, a theory he had to believe. If Tess knew something...knew the murderer... and hadn't told Burton...

This was stupid, he thought, struggling to push down the emotions that seemed determined to bring him weeping to his knees.

Why didn't you talk to me, Tess? Why didn't you tell me what you saw? I would've saved you. Why didn't you trust me?

He pushed thoughts of her away, and instead concentrated on the feeling of the sun on his shirt back, the cold breeze playing with his hair. He tried to feel how the three women must have felt that afternoon. To have made that treacherous thirty-minute, conversation-inhibiting, trail ride---single file, butt to nose--only to arrive at a nonpicturesque clearing that they must have seen many times before, and then to argue bitterly among themselves.

A faint scent of rotting earth wafted across the breeze. From where he sat, towering above the bushes and clumps of trampled grass, he could easily see the beginning of the trail that marked the circular route back to the barn. It seemed less traveled--if that was possible--than the one he had taken to arrive at the clearing. Although it was a more logical trail for the three to have returned to the barn by, both Tess and Portia had insisted that they hadn't taken it, but had turned back and followed the trail they'd come by. Now, faced with the prospect of returning to the barn by the way he'd come, Burton again experienced the niggling in his mind. This time it rushed to the forefront in a dramatic display of instinct.

The women hadn't returned to the barn the way they said they had.

He suddenly knew this as clearly as if he'd just watched a videotape of them entering the mouth of the circular trail.

It wasn't a logical or natural option, to return via the way he'd come. It was an ugly trail and--if the map they'd been given earlier was correct-- was a less direct way back to the barn. Burton moved toward the new trail.

Why had he and Kazmaroff simply accepted their word that they hadn't taken this trail? Because it looked, at first glance, to be impassable or difficult? He twisted in the saddle and looked at the opening of the trail he'd just ridden on. It flowed into the clearing with few trees or branches flanking its sides, giving the impression that the whole of the trail was like that, open and spacious, green and pretty. Burton knew differently.

He turned back to the new trail. Perhaps this was just as deceiving in looks, he thought. He gave Best-Boy a squeeze with his knees and the horse entered the trail without hesitation. Narrow at first, the trail soon widened comfortably. There was room now for a canter or even a gallop if one had a little riding skill, Burton thought.

He re-ran his memory tapes to find the reason the women gave for not taking this trail. He put Best-Boy into a trot and rode the bounces and jolts comfortably in the big saddle, without bothering to try to post. The trail widened further and the red clay and grass soon turned into hard-packed dirt. Burton slowed when he saw tire marks join the trail.

Of course! This is where the groundskeeper lives, Lint. Burton rode further down the trail until it emptied into another clearing, much smaller this time. Parked under the pine and spruce trees was a dilapidated, but clearly inhabited trailer.

Burton stopped his horse.

And we dismissed this bit of information as being unimportant.

Why? he wondered as he dismounted. First, because Lint had an alibi, provided by Margo who swore she was in conference with the man during the time of the murder. And, second, because his footprint hadn't matched the one they'd found at the murder scene.

Burton kept his horse's reins tightly in one hand as he approached the trailer. So Lint had been eliminated as a suspect, and the two women believed because, after all, they were women and their expressing distaste at having to ride near where an odious old retard lived seemed perfectly legitimate to a couple of male chauvinist dunderheads like him and Kaz.

Yet Burton knew, without doubt, that this was the way Portia and Tess had come.

He tied Best-Boy's reins to a bush, ignoring Margo's earlier warning that these horses were not Western ponies and the rules of Bonanza did not apply. He crept silently up to the trailer.

As he neared, he could hear muffled voices rising and falling naturally in conversation. He peered through the dirty window of the trailer and immediately saw Bill Lint, his back to Burton, working at a small hot plate. The man was short and stocky. His shoulders seemed muscular through his thin plaid shirt as he stirred a frying pan on the coil. Quickly, Burton looked around the trailer interior for Lint's companion. She sat quietly on the couch, across from the window. Burton caught his breath. Not only was the woman completely naked, she was staring directly at him. One hand supported her head in a casual display of insouciance -- a head covered in long blonde hair and coated in large, brown splotches of dried blood. She didn't move, her long eyelashes didn't blink or flutter.

Lint continued to converse brightly as he cooked. Burton stood up slowly from his crouching position and stared in horror and mounting nausea at the woman seated on the couch.

It was Jilly.

Chapter Ten

1

Burton kicked in the aluminum door to the trailer. He held his gun in front of him with both hands, the nose of it pointed slightly downward.

"Freeze!" He barked. "Put your hands where I can see them." Right away, the odor from the body--visibly decomposing even at ten feet away--began to overpower Burton.

Lint jumped violently, dropping the frying pan on the floor. Onions and garlic and green peppers spilled across the chipped and peeled linoleum.

The combined smell of frying foods and the rotting corpse assaulted Burton like a weapon. Gagging, and resisting the urge to cover his nose, he grabbed Lint by the shirt and yanked him out of the trailer.

Immediately, Burton gasped in great draughts of fresh air, his gun poised on Lint.

The groundskeeper glared at Burton from under a slightly bowed head and thick eyebrows. He kept his hands in the air.

"I ain't done nothing," he said. "Margo said I could cook. She done give me that hot plate--"

The man reeked of garlic. Under the scent lay a more pervasive, and considerably nastier aroma.

Burton read the man his rights.

"You can say anything you want," Lint said, lowering his hands. "I ain't done nothin' wrong."

"Move away from the trailer." Burton wagged his gun in the direction toward the main barn. "Put your hands on top of your head. Where's your car?"

"Don't got no car."

"You're lying. I see tire tracks."

"Don't got no car!"

"What's the matter, Lint? Was Jilly mean to you? Jilly call you bad names? That why you killed her?"

Lint lowered his hands.

"I didn't kill Jilly," he said.

"Put your hands back up and turn around. So, she just drop in for lunch...naked and dead?"

"I didn't kill Jilly," Lint repeated. "She's my girlfriend. I wouldn't hurt her none."

Not sure I want to hear where this is going.

"How is it, then, that you got her stinking, rotting body propped up on your couch?"

Lint whirled around, his hands in fists.

"Don't talk about her like that?"

"Careful, bud." Burton motioned him to put his hands back.

Lint ignored him.

"Jilly had a little accident," Lint said. "I found her hurting. I fixed her up. She wants to live with me now. She says I'm her main boyfriend..."

"Did you also find her without any clothes on?"

"Don't talk dirty about her! I'm her main boyfriend! I'm the one she wants!"

"Yeah, okay...Bill, right? Your first name's Bill?"

Lint nodded.

"Just stay put." Burton shifted his Glock semi-automatic to one hand and reached into his jacket for his cell phone. "But do it down wind over there."

2

"Well, I appreciate your concern, but, really, I think I'm quite safe." Portia sat primly across from Detective Kazmaroff, a coffee table full of china cups and creamers between them.

"My partner and I feel that may not be absolutely the case," Kazmaroff said, taking a sip of the hot tea.

Portia pushed a glossy lock of blonde hair back from her face. She wore a voluptuous Dolce & Gabbana knit dress, revealing her excellent figure and a good deal of cleavage.

"Well, I can't imagine--" she started.

"You see, Mrs. Stephens..." Dave set his cup down and flipped open his notebook. "It seems that when we went through Tess's...Miss Andersen's things...we found a note that fairly clearly involves her in Jilly's murder--"

"I...I don't believe you!" Portia's hand flew to her mouth. It trembled noticeably.

"In fact, the note is very specific about the details of that last ride with the three of you..."

"Tess would never have left such a note!"

"I don't think Miss Andersen expected to be checking out quite so soon," Kazmaroff said, smiling. "Are there more cookies?"

Portia pulled on the rings on her fingers and rubbed her hands together in agitation.

"She didn't mention me in the note?" she asked, unhappily.

"Well, actually, yes, she did," Kazmaroff said. "Not only did Miss Andersen confess to killing Jilly...something I guess you've known all along...but she said you were an accomplice to--"

"It's a lie!" Portia stood up. "It's a foul lie! I had nothing to do with it!"

"Well, Miss Andersen wrote--"

"I don't care what Tess wrote! It isn't true!"

"You knew what Tess intended to do in the clearing."

"Scare Jilly! That's all I knew she intended to do."

"I don't believe you, Mrs. Stephens."

"Scare her! Scare her! That's all! She said they were going to play a joke on her!"

"'They'?"

"They...Tess and the guy." Portia sat back down and put her face, so carefully made up, in her hands.

"Who was the guy?"

"I have no idea. I heard them talking after I left the clearing. I heard the guy's voice and then...well, then, Jilly screaming...so I just raced back to the barn as fast as I could. Zanzibar even got a nasty scratch across his left flank. Later, Tess said it all went horribly wrong."

"More for some than others," Kazmaroff said.

Portia looked up at him.

"Did Tess really leave a note?"

"Really? No."

Portia held herself very straight, her hands gripped tightly in her lap. She blew out a long breath, then hung her head like a marionette collapsing after a performance.

"Does it make me an accomplice if I thought they were just going to scare her but it didn't work out that way?" she whispered.

"You've been withholding information."

"I was afraid."

Kazmaroff smiled at the maid bringing in a fresh plate of cookies.

"You should be," he said.

3

Burton put his cell phone away. His hunch about Portia had been correct. All the pieces were finally beginning to fall together. All but the footprint, and perhaps that could be explained once he and Kazmaroff laid out all the evidence and clues in logical order. He looked at Lint, who was huddled in a crouch by a tree picking pine needles out of his socks.

We got Jilly's body, and we know who killed her. It's just a matter now of making all roads lead to the right spot.

"My friends will be here soon," Burton said.

"You don't have to talk down to me," Lint said sullenly. "I know you're a cop."

"Yes, well, then, my *cop* friends will be here soon." Burton walked to the trailer. He felt he should cover her but a part of him rationalized that it didn't really matter.

Instantly, Lint was on his feet.

"Where you going?" he demanded.

"You got a bedspread or something for Miss Jilly?" Burton asked, holding a handkerchief to his face and peering into the trailer.

"She don't like to be too hot!" Lint's voice began to rise.

"Why doesn't that surprise me?" Burton muttered, as he took a step into the trailer. He spotted a stained afghan across one of the chairs. He turned to call to Lint: "I'm just going to--"

The blow hit him hard across the temple.

4

The policemen hoisted Mark Travers, screaming and kicking, into the jail cell.

"I want my lawyer! You can't do this to me! I'll see you bastards lose your badges!"

One of the cops boxed Travers on the ear.

"Shut-up, ass-hole. Unless you want to wake up your new sleeping partners." They turned and left, clanging the jail door loudly as if they intended to do just that.

Travers gripped the bars and pressed his face into them.

"I want my lawyer!" he wailed.

"Hey, knock it off!" a voice growled to him from the interior of the cell.

Mark whimpered and dared a look over his shoulder in the direction of the voice.

Another voice chimed in:

"Yeah, it ain't so bad. It's just overnight, right?"

Travers turned around and tried to make out the shapes of his companions in the dark.

"You guys in here just for the night, too?" he asked, relaxing somewhat as he envisioned a group of sleepy deadbeat dads and DUIs.

"Oh, yeah," one of the voices said, laughing. "Just one night. Besides, usually, that's all it takes, lover."

More voices joined in on the mounting laughter.

5

The first thing Burton saw when he awoke, was Best-Boy's feet. His head exploding in pain, he rolled away from the massive animal's hooves and sat up.

Stupid! What were you doing? Protecting Jilly's modesty or something?

His hand flew to his shoulder holster and he expelled a sigh of relief. His gun was there. Quickly, he scanned the clearing. No sign of Lint. He jogged over to the trailer and peered in the door. The interior of the trailer didn't smell as bad. Probably because Jilly's corpse had been removed.

Cursing, he turned back to the horse and gathered up the reins. Just as he was about to swing up into the saddle, he heard singing.

Burton drew his gun and held it straight down at his side. He walked carefully in the direction of the voice, lilting up and down melodically, a nonsense tune, like one being made up as the singer goes along.

He edged around the trailer. There, an old Dodge Valiant was parked on gravel and dirt. Leaning against the fender was a shot gun. The passenger door was open but no one was visible. He paused, watching the car, trying to decide what to do next.

Suddenly, Lint came from out of the bushes, carrying Jilly's body in his arms. He'd partially covered her in the bedspread. As Lint approached the car, obviously intending to put the corpse into it, he scraped his load against a pine tree. Burton watched one of Jilly's pale, slim arms detach and flop to the ground. Lint cursed.

Burton moved out of the shadows and pointed his gun at Lint.

"Put it down," he said loudly.

Lint seemed to flinch at the sound of Burton's voice. He hesitated.

"Do it now!" shrieked Burton. He didn't want Lint getting any closer to the car and the shotgun.

Lint began a slow squat with the body in his arms. Burton could see Jilly's eyes staring unseeing up to the fair November sky. He seemed to be resisting any separation from the body. Suddenly, he dumped it on the ground, revealing a small dove-hunting rifle, which he raised and fired at Burton.

6

Kazmaroff sped down the tractor-road leading to the barn. He snapped shut his cell phone and tossed it in the passenger seat.

Burton wasn't answering, and their back-up was still trying to negotiate the evening-before-Thanksgiving traffic.

He, himself, would also be sitting on Peachtree Industrial Road if he hadn't been at Portia Stephen's house-- just a few miles north of the barn.

Why wasn't he answering?

Kazmaroff accelerated, sending up a choking veil of dust and dirt on the road behind him.

7

The bullet tore into Burton's shoulder. He felt the fire explode down his whole left side as he flung himself to the ground, firing his Glock semi-automatic as he went down. Amid the pounding thunder of the blood rushing to his head and the report of his own gun, he could hear the sounds of police sirens as if they are coming from far away. He could also hear that Lint was still shooting.

Twisting on the ground in pain and in search for cover, Burton fired off two more rounds, then scrambled into a thorny bush. He didn't feel the merciless brambles tear into his clothes and skin. He held his breath and listened. It was quiet.

On the ground in front of Jilly's body, lay Lint. The spreading crimson pool surrounding both him and the other body like a conspiratorial hug.

Slowly, agonizingly, Burton extricated himself from the shrub. He held his left arm carefully against his chest, aware that the wound seemed to have stopped bleeding. It still hurt like hell.

He stood over Lint, then squatted and touched the man on the neck, looking for the carotid artery.

"Jesus!" A voice came out of the wilderness.

Burton looked up to see Dave Kazmaroff jerk open his car door and run across the clearing to him. Jack hadn't even heard the car drive up.

His second thought as he watched his burly partner briefly examine the bodies and begin talking into his cell phone, was relief that he was there to take over.

His first thought was that he'd be damned if he'd pass out in front of him.

Chapter Eleven

1

Kazmaroff pulled up in front of Jack Burton's house and idled the car, waiting while Burton collected himself.

"So, the doc said it's just a scratch?" he peered into the rear view mirror. A few of Burton's neighbors were standing in the street.

Burton grunted.

"It's no big deal," he said. "It just chipped me. It'll heal by Christmas. Thanks for the ride."

"Yeah, no problem," Dave said. "I don't have Thanksgiving Day plans either." He indicated Burton's dark, obviously unoccupied, house with a jerk of his head.

Burton decided to let it go and get out of the car before the drugs wore off. He swung open the door, careful not to jar his bandaged left shoulder.

"The Chief says it's a collar," Kazmaroff said.

Burton hesitated.

"Well, it's certainly something," he said.

"No, man, he says we got him. He's very happy."

"When did you talk to the Chief?"

"While you were in the Emergency room."

"The footprint doesn't fit Lint."

Kazmaroff frowned.

"You telling me you don't think Lint killed Jilly?" he asked, turning in the drivers seat to face Burton.

Burton sat in the car as if dredging up the strength to get out. He stared through the windscreen.

If not Lint, than who?

"I'm saying I'm tired," he said. "And the little pills the doc gave me have definitely kicked in." Burton edged out of the car and closed the car door with his foot. He tottered on the curb for a moment, looking at his unlighted, unwelcoming home. Two of his neighbors walked by and he nodded a greeting to them.

When they passed, he looked at Kazmaroff through the passenger's side window.

"And the footprint doesn't fit Lint."

2

The next morning was Thanksgiving Day and it shone bright and clear at Bon Chance Stables. The sunlight was sharp and the wind was nippy. Just the way Margo liked it for an autumn hack in the woods.

Unfortunately, that's not in the cards, she thought as she brushed Beckett, her quarter horse. Her ribs were still too sore to do any riding. It had taken her a full fifteen minutes just to get his sheet off him. And now, instead of neatly folded at the corners and draped over his stall front, it lay in a tangled hill of waterproof canvas where she'd tossed it in the tack room.

The other horses were still in the pasture. She was late calling them in for their breakfast. Normally, she'd have had Beckett groomed-- and exercised!--and all the stall-boarders munching quietly in each of their stalls by now.

Hell, normally, Jessie would've done it.

But it was Thanksgiving Day, and even Jessie had some other place to go; some group of people she called family who wanted to see her, demanded her presence at their holiday table.

Margo grimaced and tossed the dandy brush into her open tack trunk. She had Beckett tied in front of the wash stand in the open end of the north barn. From here she could see the entire barn complex to the south, and the undulating, brown hills and scrub pasture to the north and north east.

Imagine, she thought, staring at the hill, dotted with spiky Georgia pines. Every time she'd endured that idiot in the last week...every time she'd given him an order, patiently explained something to him, or simply suffered his malodorous presence--he'd later gone back to that trailer of his on the south loop of the polo pasture trail and made love to Jilly's dead body.

Margo rubbed her eyes with a tired hand. The exertion of grooming Beckett had been too much. Her arm trembled.

And now Bill was dead, too. Jilly and Tess and Bill.

Margo sat down on an upturned rubber bucket. Beckett turned his head to look at her.

So was it Bill who had tried to kill her? Bill, who had drugged Traveler? That didn't make sense!

Margo touched Beckett on his flank and the spot quivered beneath her fingers.

If Bill was in love with Jilly and thought the only way he could get her to cooperate was to kill her first, well, Margo could see that. But why kill Margo, too? She had certainly not suspected him. And she wasn't *that* tough on him!

Margo stood up and massaged the small of her back. Her ribs complained loudly. It was time to feed the horses. She debated putting Beckett in the pasture and decided she didn't have the energy to walk him to the pasture gate. She gathered Beckett's lead and took him back to his stall. She slipped the halter off his head, and locked the stall gate between them.

After she had filled the feed buckets in each of the stalls and whistled for the herd in the paddock, she watched them thunder into the barn, thirty horses, each unerringly dashing into his or her own stall. She locked the southend of the barn so they couldn't return to the pasture after feeding and then walked slowly back to her trailer. The fatigue and the ache in her chest and arms seemed overwhelming. As she walked, she found herself noting once more how she had never seen the barn so quiet or so deserted. And with that observation came the thought that maybe, it was just possible, it hadn't been Bill at all.

3

"Now this is certainly better than scrubbing out gravy bowls and wondering what to do with the turkey carcass, eh?"

Robert Shue gave his wife's hand a little pat as they sat around a large dinner table at the Dunwoody Country Club.

She smiled in agreement, her eyes on their daughter who was using a fork to tunnel into a mountain of mashed potatoes on her plate.

"Daddy? Can we go to the game room after dinner?" The little girl buried a few green peas in her potato mountain.

"Certainly, darling," Shue cooed. "We'll do all the family-like activities that families do on Thanksgiving." He turned to his wife and patted her hand again. "I'm certainly feeling thankful," he said.

"It's lovely," his wife said, indicating the large elegant dining room of the country club. "But I would've been just as happy to have made dinner at home."

"Nonsense! All that work? And mess? When you can afford not to?"

"My family always had Thanksgiving Dinner at home. I guess it just feels more traditional to me." She nodded at her daughter who was begging to be excused to talk with a school mate three tables over.

"'Your family,'" Shue sneered, then caught himself. It wasn't really her family he loathed, after all. Just that bastard of a fucking snob brother of hers.

"Your brother took *his* family here last year," he reminded her. "You didn't think it was breaking with tradition then."

His wife sighed.

"I guess I'm talking about when we were children," she said quietly, almost a whisper.

"Oh, yeah, the fucking Waltons. I forgot." Shue reached for his wine glass and then stopped. "Hey, sweetheart," he said, reaching for her hand instead. "I don't want to fight. I'm so happy about us--you know, as a family--and I've got so much to be thankful for...mostly you and Chelsea, you know?"

His wife smiled and nodded.

"I'm just so grateful for you, babe. You know that, don't you? You know how much I love you and how happy I am?"

"I know, Bob. Me, too."

"Yeah, great. Great." He drank his wine.

The server came by and refilled their water glasses. She caught his eye to silently inquire about another bottle of wine. He nodded, adding a wink. Beautiful eyes, he thought, still watching her as she moved to the next table. Beautiful everything else, too. He'd have to ask Barry who she was. Barry hired all the waitstaff.

"I've had enough, Bob."

"Huh?"

"Wine. I don't know why you ordered more. I've had enough."

"Never enough, babe." Shue licked his lips. "It's Thanksgiving."

4

It looked edible. But Burton knew the contents of his refrigerator when Dana was out of town could be, and frequently were, deceiving.

He closed the refrigerator door without taking anything out, and stood for a moment looking at all the magnets and little notes stuck to it. Pizza deliveries, reminders on library books that had been returned weeks ago, newspaper clippings. He touched one of the clippings and read the headline: *"Atlanta Humane Society Destroys 20,000 Companion Animals Each Month."* Why would Dana have this on the refrigerator, he wondered? Did she want a dog? He shook his head and tugged the clipping off its magnet. He scanned the article standing in his stocking feet in the small galley kitchen, then tossed it on the counter.

He opened the refrigerator again, had no better luck in finding something edible, and went to the kitchen pantry. After sorting through open cracker boxes and a couple jars of rice and beans, he found a few ancient Poptarts which he inserted into a wide-slotted bagel toaster he found under the sink. While he was waiting for the pastries to toast, he stared out the front window of the house. He watched one of his neighbors walking his dog. The man edged along Burton's small, scraggly lawn with his animal--a small, fuzzy thing, looking to Burton like a cross between a diseased lamb and a Tasmanian devil. Burton found himself wondering if it were a foundling or if his neighbor had actually paid money for it.

The toaster popped up his Thanksgiving Day dinner and he turned his attention from the street back to the kitchen.

Kaz had said that Portia admitted that a man had been in the clearing with Tess at the time of the murder. She told Kaz that she had heard a man's voice. But she'd never said she'd heard *Lint's* voice. Wouldn't she have recognized Lint's voice? If it had been him?

Burton put his hand on the kitchen phone. For a moment, he seemed unsure of whom he intended to call. An image of his wife's face flashed in his mind. He pictured her laughing, sitting down to dinner with her family in Florida. He tried to remember the last time he saw her laugh in Atlanta. He glanced at the clock, wondering if his in-laws were still dining or had finished. He punched in a phone number.

"Yeah?"

"You always answer the phone like that?"

"I do on Thanksgiving Day. Fucking telemarketers never take a holiday. What's up?"

"Portia never said the voice she heard was Lint's?"

There was a pause on the line before Kazmaroff answered.

"She just said a man's voice."

"Is it weird she wouldn't have recognized his voice? The guy had a voice like a strangled chicken. I don't think it was Lint she heard in the clearing."

"We got the collar--"

"Screw the collar, man! If we can't make the pieces fit, we can't make 'em fit! It's not his print, it's not his voice! Someone else was there in the clearing..."

"But Lint is the one holding the goodie bag! If he didn't kill her, what was he doing serving high tea to her, naked, in his trailer, a week later?"

"He could've just found the body. The clearing's not a hundred yards from his trailer. Then, every time we got close, he'd hide her in the muck heap. Which explains why the dogs couldn't pick up her scent to find her."

"Because by then she had acquired all kinds of lovely new scents. Like horse shit."

They were silent for a moment.

"You alone?" Burton asked.

"On Thanksgiving?" Kazmaroff laughed. "Yeah, I'm alone."

"I'll call you back." Burton hung up the phone. He dug out his notebook and redialed, reading from it.

"Stephens residence.

"This is Detective Jack Burton. I'm sorry to disturb you. May I please speak with Mrs. Stephens?"

"I'm sure I needn't remind you that this is Thanksgiving Day, Detective."

"Is this Mr. Stephens? No, sir. If you don't mind, I'd just like to ask your wife a quick question."

"I'm afraid that won't be possible," Stephens spoke with weariness in his voice. "She's not here."

"Where may I find her?" Burton asked, patiently.

"You may find her where you would any other day of the year, but where, one would have thought you might not have on Thanksgiving Day. She's at the barn, seeing her horse."

"She's riding today?"

"The barn manager called about an hour ago," Portia's husband said. "Something about Zanzibar being lame or sick or something. Portia tore out of here without obviously needing to know many details."

"Is the vet at the barn?"

"The barn manager said the vet would meet Portia at the barn."

"Did Portia talk to the barn manager?"

"No, I took the call. Rude son of a bitch, if you ask me," Stephens said. "Practically ordered me to inform Portia of Zanzibar's condition, and then hung up! As if he has anything else to do but keep tab on the horses and wander around--"

"The voice was a man's?" Burton felt a prick of alarm.

"What?"

"The barn manager's voice. It was definitely male?"

"Well, of course it was male. I just--"

"Thanks, Mr. Stephens." Burton hung up. He pulled on his running shoes, and snatched up his car keys. He waited only until he was in his car and backing out of the driveway before he punched in Detective Kazmaroff's home number.

5

Portia ran her hands down the horse's flank to his ankles. She felt for heat, for lumps, for a reaction from the horse. She stood back and looked at the animal. Her silk drawstring slacks had already gathered dirt around the hems. She'd been in such a hurry she hadn't bothered to change shoes, either, so her neat little Chanel flats were ruined, too, with tiny clumps of red clay wedged into the soles and crusted along the instep.

Has Margo flipped? There's nothing wrong with Zanzibar! Is she just lonely? Or what?

Portia patted her horse's neck, trying to keep her annoyance out of the gesture.

"Not your fault, beauty," she murmured to the horse. "I'm happy you're okay. It's just that our barn manager has gone a little nutsy and that has Mommy worried."

Portia looked around the barn. She had led her horse from his stall to the area everyone used to tack up their horses. It was a large room at the end of the barn, adjacent to the tackroom where boarders' feed and saddles were kept. The tacking up area was open on two sides, both openings large enough for three horses to walk abreast in or out of the barn. Another side shared a common wall with the last of the stalls, and the final wall featured a large opening leading to the tack room itself.

Portia snapped the knot out of the horse's lead rope and led him back into the corridor bisecting the two rows of twenty-four stalls. She lost her footing for a moment on the slippery floor straw, and leaned against Zanzibar for support.

These were definitely not the shoes for this, she thought, her annoyance rising.

She put Zanzibar into his stall and latched the gate. It was then that she noticed that none of the other gates, except Beckett's, were locked.

Boy, that's slack! Margo must've fed them and then just walked away without bothering to check their stalls! The woman was hopeless.

Busy with thoughts of strong complaint to the barn owners, Portia picked her way back to the sunny tacking-up area of the barn to collect her handbag.

As she shouldered her bag and positioned her Gucci sunglasses on her face, she squinted across the parking lot to see two figures slowly making their way to the barn.

Good. Saves me the trouble of tracking her idea. What in the world was Margo thinking of? Calling me out here for no good reason?

Portia crossed her arms and waited for the pair to reach her, her annoyance and self-righteous indignation mounting with every approaching step. It wasn't until Margo and her companion were ten yards away that Portia thought to wonder who the man might be. And finally--and in just as much confusion--why he was walking behind Margo, pointing a gun at her back.

6

"Just tell me you bothered to check his alibi." Burton drove too fast down Peachtree Industrial Boulevard. The normally tortured street was blessedly free of traffic today.

Kazmaroff braced his arms against the dash board.

"Don't kill us, Jack," he said. "Yes, I checked it."

"And it was a zero, right? It collapsed, right?"

"Yes, but what with us nailing Lint--"

"I know, I know." Burton jammed his foot hard against the accelerator pedal. "It didn't seem important at the time."

"Shouldn't I call for back-up?" Kazmaroff found himself working a nonexistent brake pedal on the passenger's side of the car.

"Not yet," Burton said. "Let's see what we find first."

7

Ned sat primly on the bale of hay in the tacking-up room, Margo's Beretta semi-automatic resting on his knees. Portia and Margo huddled together by the entrance to the stalls. One of the horse's heads poked out of the halfdoor of his stall as if curious. Portia was crying.

"So, you see," Ned said, chewing on a thread of straw. "Things have gotten way out of hand. I really don't know how they got so out of hand." He wore thin plastic gloves.

"You're crazy," Margo said.

"Maybe. But crazy with a plan. *And* crazy with a gun, too. Which beats your not-crazy with nothing." Ned giggled.

"He killed Jilly," Portia whispered loudly to Margo. "I heard his voice in the clearing."

Margo patted her shoulder.

"I know, Portia."

Ned looked around the barn, then stood up.

"We better get started on this. I imagine we have all day what with it being the holiday and all, but I got a late dinner I'm expected at."

"Where are we going?" Margo asked.

"Oh, you're not going anywhere, sweetheart," Ned said, producing a pad of notepaper and a pen. "Just a little writing assignment, is all."

"You want me to *write* something?"

"That's right." Ned tossed the paper and pen to Margo. "I'll dictate, you write."

Margo picked up the pad and pen.

"I killed Jilly Travers," Ned said.

Margo and Portia just stared at him.

"You're not writing," he said.

"You want me to take down your confession?"

Ned laughed.

"I guess I should explain," he said, with a grin. "We are creating *your* written confession to the murders of Jilly Travers and Tess Andersen."

"*My*--?" Margo shook her head in confusion.

Portia looked at Margo and edged slightly away.

"Margo? *You* killed Tess and Jilly?" she asked breathlessly.

"Even if I write it," Margo said as Ned raised his gun. "It wouldn't stand up. There's no evidence to support it. I'd just say you made me do it. It would be worthless."

"Oh, why don't you let me worry about that?"

Margo dropped the pad in the straw and dirt floor of the barn.

"No," she said.

Ned approached and pointed the gun to Portia's head.

"Permit me to change your mind," he said.

Margo hesitated, watching the man's eyes.

"Don't think I'm serious?" Ned said, his voice becoming angry. He took a step closer, then turned and pointed the gun to the head of the chestnut gelding peering out over the gate of his stall. "How 'bout now?" he said, smiling.

Margo bent down and picked up the pad.

8

The sky had turned a pewter gray with ugly streaks of copper in it. The twenty horses grazing in the pasture seemed to react at once, as if to an unseen presence. They lifted their heads from their mindless nibbling, and twitched their tails nervously. The mounting wind carried a silent message to them, along with a scattering of leaves and dust. One horse, a young bay, whirled and started. He stood, as if stunned, his eyes wide and white. Another horse screamed shrilly. They moved amongst each other in agitation now, the calm of the afternoon gone. When the sky dimmed and a silent flash of lightning flickered on the horizon, they all bolted at once. They ran in a trampling stampede of fear across the meadow and away from the terrible light, the dangerous *thing,* that threatened them all.

9

Ned smiled as he re-read the note.

"Very nice," he said.

"It won't do you any good," Margo said. She and Portia remained standing by the entrance to the horses' stalls.

"Well, thanks for humoring me, then," he said, smiling broadly.

"It'll be my word against yours," she said.

"I never really thought you killed the girls, Margo," Portia said quietly.

"Thanks, Portia," Margo said, with a sigh. She shifted her weight off her damaged ribs and cradled her broken right arm close to her chest.

"Well, actually, the only word of yours the authorities will have to go on will be this." Ned wagged the confession gaily in the air.

Margo took a step forward and Ned hastily aimed the gun in her direction.

"Yes, ladies," he said. "As I said, things had gotten out of hand. The Jilly thing I had nailed, so to speak. But when I had to do Tess Andersen too, well, my alibi couldn't keep pace." He giggled.

"You're an idiot," Margo said.

"An idiot who still has many hot meals ahead of him, unlike you."

"The police thought they got their murderer last night."

"What are you talking about?"

Margo took another step closer.

"They found Jilly's body in our groundsman's trailer yesterday. They shot and killed him. They thought...we all thought... that *Bill* killed Jilly."

Ned seemed ruffled now.

"I don't believe you," he said.

Margo waved her hand.

"All this was for nothing. You were safe, man!"

"I'm still safe!" Ned said, raising his voice. "Once I kill the two of you with your own gun, your fingerprints all over it!" He was shouting now and waving the gun at them both. Margo felt her breakfast try to come up at Ned's words. She was aware of the horses in the barn beginning to move around. She could smell a storm in the air.

"It'll look like murder-suicide," he continued. "Your note will be the finishing touch. I'll be *damn* safe, then. You can bet on it!"

Quickly, Margo tossed the handful of dirt into his eyes.

Ned flailed his arms and fired blindly.

The sound of the explosion ripped into the interior of the barn, igniting the restless horses.

Ned clawed the dirt from his eyes and tried to re-aim.

The horses charged down the center corridor of the barn towards the three people in a surge of several tons of terrified, thundering horseflesh.

10

Burton grabbed Kazmaroff and shoved him hard. The two fell in a painful tangle of arms and legs behind a skinny pine tree as the panicked hoard of thirty horses hurtled from the opening of the lower barn and careened wildly across the barn grounds.

Kazmaroff rolled off Burton and got to his feet.

"Shit!" he said, watching the horses disappear in a cloud of dust down the dirt road. "Is that normal?"

Burton yanked his partner back behind the tree and pulled his weapon.

"*Now* you can call for back-up," he said.

11

"Where are you, you bitches?!" Ned screamed, clutching the gun and pointing it everywhere his eyes darted. He ran down the middle of the stall corridor, kicking open stall doors. The dust from the stampede hadn't settled yet. It floated in small choking puffs just above the straw floor. He heard a muffled cough and whirled around.

"I've got Portia, Miss Barn Manager," he shouted. "Come out or I shoot her right now."

He heard the rustling of straw to his left and ran in the direction of the noise.

Margo picked herself up from the floor of the empty stall. Straw clung to her hair and her sling. Ned entered the stall and pointed his gun at her head. He grabbed her by the hair and jerked her out.

"Oh, sorry about the fib. I guess I didn't have Portia after all. But if it's any consolation," he said, yanking her by her hair as the two stumbled down the corridor, "I'm sure I soon will."

12

"So, what do you think's going on in there?" Kazmaroff had drawn his own weapon. They were in front of the barn, crouched behind a tree.

Burton shook his head.

"I don't know. It was definitely a gunshot we heard. And we know Portia's in there." He nodded in the direction of Portia's Mercedes in the parking lot.

"And the horses definitely *aren't*, that's for sure," Kazmaroff said.

Burton looked at him.

"Don't look at me like that, man" Kazmaroff said. "I'm just running down the situation. A hundred fucking horses come barreling down my ass--"

"You just gave me an idea," Burton said, with surprise in his voice.

13

Ned found Portia huddled in terror at the back of the tack room. He considered tying them up but realized it wouldn't look much like suicide if their hands were bound.

Portia began to cry softly.

"I could always untie you after I shot you," Ned said, holding a piece of lead rope in his hand, frowning, thinking outloud.

Portia wept louder.

"You, in the barn! This is the police!"

The shock of the booming voice made all three jump violently. Ned whirled around to the opening of the tack room and peered out. He kept his gun, shaking wildly now, pointed back at the two women seated on a dusty tack trunk against the wall of the tack room. He saw a car parked next to Portia's car that hadn't been there before. He couldn't tell where the voice was coming from.

"Drop your weapons and come out with your hands on top of your head! This is the police!"

Ned turned back to the women, his eyes wild with fear and hysteria.

"It's over, man!" Margo said. She didn't look as afraid now. More expectant. She was sitting on the trunk, holding Portia's hand. Portia had stopped crying.

"I got the note!" Ned screamed. He fired in their direction.

14

"Jesus, Jack! He's shot one of them! What took you so long?"

"I had to find a halter first," Jack said, as he led Best-Boy up to the tree.

"Forget it, man. This ain't gonna work."

"It's got to."

15

The shot hit the foot of the tack trunk and both women screamed and jumped into each other's arms.

"How else out of here?" Ned demanded.

Margo hesitated.

He had to know it was over! The police were here. Would he still kill them?

"How else! How else?!" Ned screamed, wagging the gun at them.

"The end of the corridor leads to the north pasture," Margo said.

"They'll see me as soon as I step out of this room!" Ned ran to them and held his gun against Portia's face. "Do better than that!"

"I...they can't sneak up to the barn without you seeing them," Margo said.

"I'm not worried about them taking me by surprise, you stupid bitch!" Ned bellowed. "They know I know they're here!"

"I mean..." Margo gulped and tried not to look at the gun barrel pressed to Portia's weeping face. "I mean, the way the barn's designed, they can't approach without you seeing them."

Ned lowered his gun.

"So I've got some time," he said to himself.

"You could bargain with them," Margo said. Her ribs felt like fire under her ace bandage. She wondered if she'd rebroken them with the tumble in the stall. "Make a deal."

He looked at her.

"I could still shoot your ass," he said. "And just say I interrupted you in the process of killing yourself and murdering Portia here."

Portia stopped crying for a moment.

"Only," Ned said, his humor seeming to return, "I wasn't able to prevent your deaths, simply save myself." He nodded. "Then, I've still got the note absolving me from the other murders..."

"If you're really that stupid," Margo said. "I guess I'll save my breath."

"For your prayers, lady," Ned said, bringing the gun to her mouth. "Open wide. I want to make this look good."

Suddenly, they heard a noise at the opening of the tack room. At the same time, the light in the room vanished.

Ned jerked around, his gun in front of him.

"What the--?" He pointed the gun at the behemoth animal standing in the doorway, who was blocking out the light, eliminating any chance of exit.

"It's Best-Boy," Portia whimpered.

The tack room was nearly dark now.

"What's he doing here?" Ned asked, the frantic tenor creeping back into his voice. He looked to where Margo had been seated. He saw shadowy towers and ghostly piles of what he knew were feed sacks and grain barrels.

"Get him away from the door!" he said, firing into the semi-darkness. He heard the bullet strike wood. Desperately, he turned back to the horse in the doorway and fired his gun into its dark, looming shape.

Immediately, Best-Boy groaned and fell, allowing a burst of strong sunlight to flood the little windowless room. Ned stood in the doorway as the animal thrashed in agony at his feet. The relief at being able to see again was instantly quelled by the image of a man standing on the other side of the prostrate horse, his gun raised in both hands and pointed directly at Ned.

"Drop the gun!" The man yelled.

Ned hesitated. His own gun was already raised.

He could say he thought the cop was Margo's accomplice!

His finger touched the trigger.

He could say he was terrified by what he had just been--

He felt the sharp sensation of the snout of a gun press firmly to his temple as a second man stepped from the shadows.

"Do it," the man said.

Chapter Twelve

1

"You know, there are a couple of different interpretations of the statement 'Do it.'"

Burton spoke from the large leather chair situated in the Chief's office. It was the morning after Ned Potsak's arrest. "I mean, it could mean, 'yeah, do it--what my partner said, drop the gun'...or it could mean 'do it', as in, 'go ahead and shoot him'."

"Oh, for crying out loud." Kazmaroff rolled his eyes.

"I'm just saying," Burton continued, "...In the future...when you've got a suspect who's a little agitated and not thinking straight as it is...I'd appreciate you sticking to the book a little closer....'Freeze!' Or 'Drop your weapon!'...something unconfusable, like that."

"I'll remember that next time I'm saving your life, Jack."

Jack fought to control his temper. "Well, how about next time," he said tightly, "*you* stand in the line of fire, and *I'll* get the drop on the perp? That would probably solve this little insecurity of mine...."

"What ever you say, buddy."

The Chief entered the room, clapped Burton on the shoulder--surprising both men--and tossed a pile of folders on his desk.

"Excellent work!" he said, seating himself at the desk. "I just read your report. Excellent work."

The two mumbled their acknowledgments.

"It's hard to believe the two of you say you can't work together," he continued. "I'd like you to consider seeing the department psychologist." At the men's horrified looks, the Chief motioned with his hands in a 'calm-down' gesture. "Just a little couples counseling, that's all," he said. "I'll respect your decision if you decide against it, but I believe it's for the good of the department to keep you two working together." He grinned broadly, further convincing them that he'd slipped a cog.

"So, what do you say?"

2

It was the week before Christmas. The fog rose from the banks of the Chattahoochee in gauzy puffs. In summer, the adjacent riding trail formed a dark leafy tunnel, cool and shaded even in the blistering Southern sun. Now, the branches on the sycamores and oaks were bare, like a series of dun-colored skeletons through which one could see far down the winding trail.

"You can see all the new development now," Margo said, as she and Burton rode in single-file down the trail. "Once, Tess and I were riding around here and we ended up right under someone's bathroom window while they were in the shower. I honestly don't know who was more upset, us or them."

She turned gingerly in the saddle for his reaction.

He squeezed the sides of Tess's horse, Wizard, and trotted up to join Margo.

"You probably just added to his pastoral-living experience," he said. "Whoever it was could tell the people at the office that day: 'Wow, we actually have fox hunts right outside our bathroom window!'"

"Yeah, you're probably right." She watched him. "You're a good match on Wizard," she said. "How does he feel?"

"I'm not interested in buying him, Margo."

"He's for sale."

"No, thanks."

"Oh, well."

They rode silently for a few minutes until they came to the edge of the river. Margo gazed at the fog hovering over the river like a layer of gray chiffon. She patted her horse's neck.

"I'm ready when you are," she said.

"Not much you don't know," Burton answered.

"Who the hell was he? I don't know that. Why me? I don't know that, either."

Burton cleared his throat, watching his horse's ears prick backward to pick up a possible order from him.

"His name is Ned Potsak," he said. "He was a corporate accountant downtown in a Big Four firm, engaged to a copywriter in Jilly's ad agency."

"Well, I guess that explains it," Margo said.

Burton grinned at her.

"Settle down, Margo," he said. "Have you taken your pain medication today?"

"I don't need it any more, thank you. Continue."

"Well, Ned had slept with Jilly, it turns out."

Margo made a noise of disgust. Burton gave her a questioning look and she shook her head.

"It's just...I never understood why Jilly slept with everyone she ever met, you know?" she said. "God! I mean, was she looking for love, do you think?"

Burton politely didn't answer.

"Never mind," Margo said. "Go on."

"The bottom line for Ned," Burton said. "Was his engagement to Kathy Sue. Her family's loaded and Ned wasn't keen on upsetting her to the point where she might break off their engagement."

"He killed Jilly to keep their affair a secret?"

"Well, it really wasn't much of an affair," Burton said. "More like a one-night stand. And I don't think he would've been driven to such drastic measures but you know Jilly. She goaded him, it seems. Threatened to tell Kathy Sue. And, as a result, a situation that might not have seemed too unmanageable to Ned quickly turned into something --in his mind--more serious."

"Was Jilly blackmailing him?"

"In a way, yes. I don't think Jilly was after money. It appears that she was doing it just...you know..."

"For the sport."

They were quiet a moment.

"I wish I could see what you loved about her," Burton said.

Margo blinked back tears as she stared at the river, then leaned over and touched Burton on the arm.

"If it's any consolation," she said. "I can definitely see what Tess loved about you."

Later, as they made their way back to the barn, Burton noticed a small red-tailed fox frozen in place behind a bush. He pointed it out to Margo. The animal's eyes blinked rapidly several times and the two riders left it in peace.

Margo winced as she reached over from horseback to open the gate.

"Here, let me get that," Burton said. "Ribs are the last thing to heal." He edged Wizard to the gate, unlatched it and pushed the door forward. After the two had passed through, he shook his foot free of his stirrup and kicked the gate shut. It latched automatically but both horses jumped at the sound of the gate banging shut.

Margo laughed.

"Well, that's one way to do it," she said.

"That's not the way it's done?" Burton asked innocently.

"Let's just say it smacks of standard police procedure," she said, her smile fading.

"You're thinking of Best-Boy," Burton said, walking his horse back to her side. The trail was wide enough to afford the two to walk abreast now. "The idea wasn't to have him get shot, you know."

"You knew he might get shot."

"I did."

"He was such a magnificent animal."

"And he's still a magnificent animal," Burton pointed out. "Didn't the vet say there's a good chance he'll be okay? Big brute like that, I'm surprised one shot could bring him down."

"I still can't believe that guy wanted to kill us. Which brings me to my next question. Why did he poison Traveler? And why did he want me dead?"

"He thought Traveler was Tess's horse."

"Traveler?" Margo looked at Burton in astonishment. "Traveler is a mixed breed!"

Burton laughed.

"Yeah, well, maybe it's just as well Tess isn't here to learn someone mistook the elderly pasture mutt for her horse."

Margo considered this for a moment, as if deciding how to react, and then smiled.

"Anyway," Burton said. "It wasn't you he was after at that point, it was Tess."

"Did Tess help him kill Jilly?"

Burton shook his head.

"I'm always going to believe it was unintentional," he said. "It seems she and Jilly had gotten into a bad habit of playing nasty tricks on each other. It certainly wasn't much of a friendship.

"Anyway, she and Ned connected--we'll probably never know how--and he offered his willingness to scare Jilly. Potsak isn't being terribly forthcoming about what the original plan was. Portia insists Tess thought it was to be only a scare."

"But, instead of scaring Jilly, Ned killed her," Margo grimaced and reshifted her position in the saddle.

"You okay?"

Margo nodded. "And Tess saw it, right?"

"And so he killed Tess, too," Burton said. "As far as your attack goes, Ned knew nothing about horses, so he got the wrong horse. And the wrong girl."

"Ouch."

"You know what I meant."

The trail turned into brown pasture. A few grazing horses lifted their heads as they rode past; most ignored them. Burton could see the roof of the barn.

"What will happen to Mark?" Margo asked.

"You still interested in him?"

"You asking this professionally or personally?"

Burton shrugged.

"The case is closed, Margo," he said. "I don't like him. So I don't like to see you with him."

Margo grinned again.

"I really don't know what to make of you, Detective," she said. "Answer my question, please."

"He's being held as a result of that little involvement with a hit man. The police really do tend to frown on contract murders." He watched Margo's face. "I mean to get an indictment, put him away for a bit, if I can. Won't be anything too serious if you're intending to wait for him or something."

"I'm not."

"Good."

The entered the last bracket of gates separating the pastures from the barn grounds and walked single file back to the barn to untack.

"One last question."

"Shoot. Metaphorically, of course."

"Poor old Bill. What was he doing with Jilly and why'd he get killed?'

Burton sighed.

"He'd obviously found Jilly soon after the murder, well, either dead or dying...and took her back to his trailer."

"But you guys had bloodhounds all over the place! Why is it you never found her at his place?"

"He stashed her in the muck heap until the dogs left."

"God Almighty."

"I shot him because he shot me. I feel sorry about that."

"Yeah, well." Margo put a hand to her temples as if to contain a thought or caress a pressure point.

"As far as what he was doing with Jilly..."

"Never mind, Jack."

As they neared the barn, they passed the riding ring where Burton pulled up.

"Whoa! Hey, Margo, is that who I think it is?"

Margo turned in her saddle to look in the direction of the ring.

"Oh, yeah, didn't I tell you?" she said. "Want to go say 'hello'?"

Burton was already trotting to the ring.

Jessie stood in the middle of the ring. She wore tight jeans and knee-high riding boots. Her long hair was caught in a ribbon and draped down her back like a yellow plume. In her hands she held a white lunge line, the end of which was attached to the bridle of one of the barn's larger lesson horses, a homely Appaloosa named Lightning.

Justin sat perched on the horse, his knees drawn too far up to be comfortable, his hands alternately gripping the pommel and the reins.

"Well, I'll be damned," Burton said as he trotted into the ring.

"Hello, Detective Burton," Jessie sang out. "Doesn't Justin look great? And whoooooaaaaa!" Jessie spoke both to Burton and the horse.

Margo walked her horse into the ring and dismounted. She slid to a standing position on the sandy ground with an audible groan.

"Justin's decided to keep Best-Boy," Margo said. "After he's recovered, and Justin's taken a few lessons, we think they might actually be a pretty good match."

"Really?" Burton looked at the boy with surprise. "Hey, kid. How's it going?"

Justin patted his mount's neck and shrugged.

"So-so," he said.

"Bull-shit!" Jessie said, laughing. "He's terrific. You got a great seat, Justin!"

Justin blushed and smiled.

Burton looked down at Margo.

"Looks like you got everything under control," he said.

"Some loose ends you just can't leave dangling," she said, not looking at him.

"Yeah, and some people are better at tying them up, too. Good for you, Margo. You got a good heart."

"Yeah, well." Margo looked uncomfortable but pleased at the praise. "What about you? We going to see you ever again or is this the good-bye-ride?"

Burton ran his fingers through Wizard's mane. The animal had been extremely responsive to him. He understood why the money added up for a horse this well-trained and obedient.

"Oh, I imagine you'll see me again," he said.

"Got plans for Christmas?" Margo asked, a little hopefully, it seemed to Burton. "I noticed you were free for Thanksgiving."

"Yeah, well, my wife's cooking dinner. You know," Jack said.

Margo turned back to the two young people in the ring.

"Oh, good," she said. "That's good. You ought to bring her out sometime. Way to go, Justin!"

Burton patted Wizard on the neck. Three mangy barn sparrows, ruffled and scrappy-looking, lined up on the fence rail of the riding ring as if ready to deliver a judgment.

Time to head back.

ABOUT THE AUTHOR

Susan Kiernan-Lewis lives in Atlanta and writes about horses, France, mysteries and romance. A freelance writer and advertising copywriter, she is also an amateur filmmaker.

Like many indie authors, Susan depends on the reviews and word of mouth referrals of her readers. If you enjoyed *Walk Trot Die,* please consider leaving a review saying so on Amazon.com, Barnesandnoble.com or Goodreads.com. Go to Susan's website at susankiernanlewis.wordpress.com and feel free to contact her at sanmarcopress@me.com.